PLANET OF THE ORCS

NOVEL

II

WRITTEN BY

HIMATARO ZUKUNASHI

Airship

Seven Seas Entertainment

Seven Seas press and purchase enquiries can be sent to Marketing Manager Lianne Sentar at press@gomanga.com. Information regarding the distribution and purchase of digital editions is available from Digital Manager CK Russell at digital@gomanga.com.

Follow Seven Seas Entertainment online at sevenseasentertainment.com.

TRANSLATION: Roy Nukia
ADAPTATION: Jeffrey Thomas
COVER DESIGN: Nicky Lim
INTERIOR LAYOUT & DESIGN: Clay Gardner
COPY EDITOR: Meg van Huygen
LIGHT NOVEL EDITOR: T. Anne
PREPRESS TECHNICIAN: Melanie Ujimori
PRINT MANAGER: Rhiannon Rasmussen-Silverstein
PRODUCTION MANAGER: Lissa Pattillo
MANAGING EDITOR: Julie Davis
ASSOCIATE PUBLISHER: Adam Arnold
PUBLISHER: Jason DeAngelis

ISBN: 978-1-64827-626-2
Printed in Canada
First Printing: February 2022
10 9 8 7 6 5 4 3 2 1

CONTENTS

CHAPTER 1

The Curse and the White Dragon

IT HAPPENED in the margrave's city, on the northernmost border.

A cup of Bago tea brewed by a junior officer sat steaming on the table. The chief accountant was about to reach for it, but before he could do so, his nearby subordinate claimed the cup for himself. Nevertheless, the chief said nothing about his subordinate's lack of courtesy. His assistant was an orc who was earnest beyond compare, and he was apparently quite tired, so the chief accountant only watched silently as he took a sip.

The second he tasted the tea, the accountant winced. It had been brewed extra strong, according to the chief's preference. As the chief let a laugh slip, the other orc shot him a glare, but his resentment was hardly justified—after all, he had been the one to steal the cup. In any case, the bitter tea was evidently enough to shock him out of his drowsiness, as he quickly returned to work with a grimace.

After asking the junior officer to fetch another cup, the chief returned his attention to the document before him. His logistics department was busier than it had ever been, and there was no time for frivolities.

Chief accountant was a surprisingly important position in the margrave's army. When the main army had sallied forth on their expedition, he had been granted the position of deputy commander and had stayed behind as the sole high-ranking official in the city. It was his job to oversee everything from logistical support to public order. If, by chance, misfortune befell the supreme commander, the chief accountant and his staff would immediately become the new commanding officers of the army, at which time his duties would shift toward rebuilding the army and defending the margrave's city from whatever had eliminated the main force.

Fortunately for him, the orc who currently served as chief accountant had never had to shoulder responsibilities of that sort. In fact, if it were to happen now, he would surely die from being overworked. He was already more than occupied with the usual yearly mobilizations, which consisted of about a third of the standing army and the militia (those soldiers who opted to live among the pioneers). This year, they had mobilized all available hands, scraping together every pioneer they could find and sending them north, making for a terrible mess.

On top of that, there'd been an abnormally high number of refugees this year. The humans used their dragons to burn down settlements from the sky, and thus, smoked out of their homes, the pioneers flooded into the margrave's city seeking beds, food, and safety. The cost of food had shot up in the blink of an eye, while public order fell into disarray just as quickly. To deal with these food shortages, they had been forced to open the doors of the army's storehouses, which meant that the expeditionary force—which had been on the verge of cornering those accursed humans—had been forced to retreat. Emergency food distribution had been added to the chief's long list of duties.

If that had been his only responsibility, he could have put up with it. He was working far beyond his pay grade, and he would be the first to call himself a slacker, but he knew his job well. Thankfully, the expeditionary force would return soon, and once that happened, he wouldn't have to worry about organizing all the supply shipments anymore.

The earnest assistant who had snatched his tea handed him a sheet to look over. A grimace settled on the chief's face as he took in the words *victory celebration*.

His understudy looked at him dubiously. "Is something wrong?"

"It's nothing. Just brought up some unpleasant memories."

This was certainly his biggest headache. In a normal year, when the pioneer militia dispersed, his only duty would be to pay each settlement for their contribution, but this year was going to be different. This year, they would hold a victory celebration, of all things. All the allied forces would gather in the margrave's city and parade down the main thoroughfare.

It was not a sensible undertaking. These festivities would do little more than use up supplies they didn't have to keep the troops fed. In addition to that, they would need to find sleeping arrangements for over fifty thousand soldiers, which was far more than the existing facilities could accommodate. Even if they had them make camp, there weren't enough empty plots of land for miles around. If they went that route, they would need to flatten farmland—at a time when there was a food shortage, no less—and pay the farmers considerable compensation for it. The chief accountant already had an idea about where he might attempt this, but negotiations were at a standstill. Worst-case scenario, he would need to put the military police to work to get it done.

Even if they overcame the challenges of arranging the victory celebration, the next issue was waiting for the troops. Most of the militia had lost their home villages, so he could no longer send their payments to each village once they had the funds. If he didn't call off their missions and pay them now, there would definitely be problems to come.

The list of issues went on. Even if they were paid for their services, the militia fighters had nowhere to go. Most would likely join the city's growing number of refugees. How would they feel once they discovered the paltry amount of bread loaves they could afford with the money they had risked their lives for? They wouldn't be pleased, that was for sure.

The chief's stomach churned and ached. He thought back to the resignation form he had filled out the other day. All he had to do was hand it in to the appropriate parties, and that would deliver him from these troubles; yet even now, it remained tucked in a corner of his desk. His health had taken an unfortunate turn as of late, and the days he'd needed to spend bedridden were growing more and more frequent. To top things off, there was no one but him left to give his idiot son a well-deserved kick to the rear.

Considering all that was to come, the chief accountant felt his spirit slipping away.

The day after His Majesty ordered me to mediate the dispute in Kerulgarz, I loaded a dragon keeper onto Veralgon's back and made for Kadann Hill. Kadann Hill was a modest bit of land consisting of just two villages and a temple, with a hill in the center that was considered sacred ground. It was about half a day from the royal capital by dragon.

Kadann Hill was the land that had been granted to me—the hero from another world. It came hand in hand with the irksome title of field marshal. This title would normally have given me control over the kingdom's entire armed forces in place of His Majesty, who was still only a minor, but as I had just arrived in this world without any personal connections, it was little more than a formality.

Kerulgarz lay south of Kadann Hill, just one territory over. The plan was to spend a night at the lord's manor in Kadann Hill before leaving early the next morning.

Having touched down in front of the stables, I handed off the reins to the keeper, who took them and gingerly led Veralgon inside. This was understandable, as Veralgon was in a foul mood. I had forced him on when he wasn't in perfect condition, carrying two riders to boot. That would've made me grumpy too.

Under normal circumstances, we would have rested several days before embarking, but there was little to be done when the king gave a direct order. He had said, "After witnessing the intensity of that white dragon, I think no one would dare oppose you." He did speak some truth. After seeing such an irritated dragon, anyone would drop their pitchfork and run for the hills.

Torson soon came from the manor to greet me. I'd sent him a message within the day to alert him of my coming, which must have arrived safely, as he didn't seem the least bit surprised. Behind him, a woman and several attendants appeared in the manor's entrance. It took a moment for me to recognize the woman as Megriel, the aspiring hero. Today, she wore riding clothes, primarily red in color. The outfit wasn't meant for women but was akin to the clothing a man might wear under his armor. The contrast between her calm childlike face and masculine crimson clothing evoked sensuality somehow.

I glanced questioningly at Torson, but he only shook his head. He evidently had no idea why she was there either. I didn't know how the news of my coming had reached her, and it would probably be in my best interest to look into it.

"It's been a while, Hero." Meg got down on one knee and offered a knightly salute. Torson retreated a step behind her and followed suit. Meg was the proxy head of her house, which put her at a higher rank than Torson, who was a royalty-appointed governor.

Once greetings had been exchanged, Meg pouted and came out with a rather incomprehensible statement. "You're getting up to some interesting things, I hear. But not a word of it to me? You don't feel bad about that?"

"What are you referring to?" I asked, and she scowled.

"That's no tone to take with a retainer who's sworn their loyalty to you," she rebuked me. So was this the proper tone for a retainer to take with her lord? I highly doubted that, but I didn't care enough to get into it.

"What's up?"

"Oh, I heard all about it! You led the dragon riders and forced the orcish armies to retreat. Didn't you promise to take me into battle with you?"

I didn't recall making that promise, but I was losing faith in my own memory, seeing how impassioned she was about this. Knowing her, though, it was possible she'd forced such a promise on me without me realizing it. It was best that I ask Torson about it later.

"I thought you'd be too busy getting your house in order," I replied. "In any case, the forces of Morsharz couldn't have played a part while the valley was sealed up. I don't think they'll have a part in the near future either."

"Really? That bites." She thought to herself for a moment, no doubt scheming something awful.

"If you want action that badly, why not become a dragon rider? Once you're able to maneuver a dragon well enough, I can put you to work as soon as you want."

At this proposal, Meg lifted her face excitedly.

It wasn't as if I'd offered it out of kindness; I had a gut feeling that keeping her close and reined in was far safer than leaving the frustrated young lady to take matters into her own hands. It would also be far more reassuring to leave the Knights of Morsharz under the supervision of her uncle, who seemed to understand common sense. On top of that, Meg had enough natural talent to casually touch Veralgon. That would surely be to her advantage.

"Yeah," she said, considering it. "Becoming history's first female dragon rider is certainly appealing..."

"Right? I bet you'd be a fine rider! Sir Rigel might oppose it, but I'm sure I could convince him." I pushed the point, since she still seemed hesitant.

"But..."

"What's stopping you?"

"That's not exactly what I want to be."

Apparently, the young lady didn't just want fame and fortune.

"I see. So what *do* you want to be?"

"I picture myself leading an army and fighting like my father. I do admire dragon riders, but there is a limit to what one fighter can accomplish on their own."

One's individual limit was something I was well aware of myself. The powers I was able to use varied depending on which world I was sent to, but even in the worlds where I could draw upon massive wells of magic, I was unable to do everything alone. This was even more evident in this world, where the mana was so thin.

While I was ruminating about this, a gleam came to Meg's eyes. "If I were to lead an army, then the powers at my disposal, the tactics available, and the freedom to act would be unlimited! I'd lead the elites of the elites into critical battles where humanity's fate hung in the balance, using the utmost of my might and ingenuity! Doesn't that get you heated just thinking about it?"

She said this with the passionate expression of a maiden in love, despite being anything but. It definitely did get me heated, but not in the way she meant. I was a gentleman visitor from a world where gender-based distinctions were fading, so I wouldn't speak of such things out loud.

Instead, I asked about our current reality. "Incidentally, what are you doing here? Have you finished uniting the lesser lords?"

"Of course!" She perked up another notch, as if she'd been waiting for that very question. "They have all sworn loyalty to my brother, of course, and to me as well. Morsharz is ready to answer the hero's call at any moment. Also..."

Meg turned and called to one of her attendants behind her. On closer inspection, I saw that her attendants were all women in masculine attire, and they were all quite stunning as well. Meg really had been doing whatever she pleased since coming into her new position.

One of the butler-like maids came forth with an item wrapped in expensive cloth and handed it to Meg. She undid the wrapping and revealed the sword and scabbard, adorned with my crest, that I had lent to her earlier.

"The lords took their oaths without any major complications, thanks to this. You can have it back now." She reverently held it out to me with gestures befitting a knight. Grinning, she said,

"Since you will be going on to Kerulgarz tomorrow, I thought it would be a good idea to have a sword on your person, so I came here as quickly as I could."

In combat, a spear of light was more than weapon enough, and it was far more convenient than a sword. However, a field marshal needed a sword at his hip for the sake of appearance in public. Swords were a symbol of power, after all. I did have a spare on me, but it made little impression without the crest and ornaments of the real deal, so I was grateful for her consideration.

The problem, however, was how she had known to meet me here. I'd received orders from His Majesty only yesterday, after all. It had taken half a day by dragon to get here, so how had she caught word of my visit?

She must have read my dubious expression because she said with a smile, "I have a lot of friends." She left it at that. I doubted I would get any more out of her, but to be fair, there were multiple ways to relay information, such as carrier pigeons.

I accepted the sword from her, looking it over to ascertain if there were any dents in the scabbard. Not that I thought she would treat the sword roughly, but it was an important ceremonial piece, so I felt I must. The scabbard seemed quite all right, but what about the weapon itself?

"You didn't chip the blade, did you?" I joked as I unsheathed it.

"Don't worry, I ground out all the nicks," she replied.

Don't worry? Why had she needed to grind the blade down? The sword had been brand-new when I'd given it to her. I wanted to ask her about this, but at the same time, I didn't want to get into it now. I slid the sword back into its scabbard after having drawn it only halfway out. I didn't know what she had used my sword for, but no doubt she had swung it in my name.

When my conversation with Meg had concluded, Torson hesitantly approached me.

"Hero, I have something to report."

"Yes, what is it?"

"I have finished removing the previous field marshal's furnishings, as ordered."

This was good news. Those uncanny orc items that the previous resident had left behind were gone now, which meant I could stay here with some peace of mind. But why did Torson look so apologetic about it?

"Did something happen?"

"Yes, well... I contacted Sir Aumas's successor and offered to hand the items over to their household, but they declined."

Of course they would. Those items were clearly cursed.

"They said I could dispose of them however I saw fit, so I tried donating them to a furniture dealer..."

Torson related how he had called in a furniture dealer he knew without going into details on the items in question. Once the merchant saw the articles he was to take, he swooned—and then fled the moment he regained consciousness.

"He always was faint of heart. Perhaps it was all a bit too intense. I know I should have warned him beforehand, but if I did, I feared he would have refused to even come. As you can tell, that approach backfired. My apologies."

From the sidelines, Meg huffed, "I'm sure he was overjoyed when he came, expecting to receive the furnishings of a field marshal. Who can blame him for reacting the way he did when those cursed things came out? I feel sorry for him."

She'd said something sensible for once. Perhaps it was going to snow.

"I have nothing to say to that." It was Torson's own fault for his dishonesty. Tricking a merchant to come here had already been enough grounds to turn down the offer.

"So where are my predecessor's belongings now?"

"I have them piled up in a corner of the estate."

Torson shot a sidelong glance at a mountain of junk.

"Why haven't you burnt them yet?" Meg made little attempt to hide her disgust. "If you don't act soon, you'll have a vengeful spirit on your hands."

When I inquired, she explained that cremation was the proper means by which to dispose of orcish bodies in this world. Otherwise, it was believed they would haunt the living and bring harm to everything around them.

Torson said, "I tried to burn them, twice. Both times, it rained. Sudden bursts of rain aren't uncommon in these parts at this time of year, but everyone's on edge thinking it's an orcish curse."

Even if it had been merely a coincidence, I couldn't blame these religious folks for seeing the downpours as some sort of hex.

"They're not yet fully dry from the last storm. I intended to check on them tomorrow to see if they were ready to try burning again."

I walked over to the heap and scanned it from top to bottom. From within the pile of ominous pieces and firewood, those taxidermied heads stared back at me. For some reason, one rolled down to my feet at that exact moment, its tongue protruding as if it were baring its fangs in laughter.

"I hope next time they burn. It would be a huge ruckus if it were to rain again," I heard Meg say to Torson forebodingly. It would indeed be viewed as a curse if burning the items failed a third time. Then again, another rain spell really wasn't out of the question.

Meg then came closer to me. "Hero."

"What?"

"Let's have Veralgon burn it down."

"I don't think we have to go that far. The smithing grass he'd need to burn this doesn't come cheap."

Veralgon's fire sack was already empty for the day. In fact, the grand dragon house's stock of smithing grass was almost completely exhausted from our scorched earth tactics. There wasn't much in general circulation, and the dragon riders' supply managers apparently had to bid against city blacksmiths in order to obtain it. Thanks to that, prices were even higher than usual.

"Kadann Hill's harvest wasn't great this year, was it?"

"True, but what's that got to do with anything?"

"If there's illness and death over the winter, they'll link it to the orc curse, no doubt about it. Then the people will turn their resentment on the lord who allowed it to happen."

"The territory's always had a shortage. That's not my fault."

"Fiefs don't always run on logic. As long as the people think it's that way, that's how it is."

I sighed, my gaze returning to that toppled head. Its expression made it seem as if it were sneering at me, taunting me. *"If you think you can burn me, just try it."* I found myself growing irritated.

"Mr. Torson, do we have any smithing grass reserves?"

"Y-yes, enough for a breath or two."

"Then tell the dragon keepers to feed Veralgon. Also, send a runner to the village chieftains."

"Very well." Torson blinked. "What do you want to tell them?"

"Tell them, 'I'll burn that junk for you. Come and watch.'"

I'd burn it right in front of their faces to allay those annoying rumors. It took a while after eating smithing grass before a dragon could breathe fire, as they required enough time to digest it in their fire sacks. By my estimation, the chieftains would arrive at just the right time.

For a moment, Torson seemed to want to say something, but then turned away to carry out my orders.

Daylight was meager in the winter days. The sun had dropped significantly by the time preparations were in order, the light around us going dim. The sky looked uncanny, with thick clouds hastening the arrival of darkness. The people who had gathered to watch the junk burn looked up at the sky anxiously. I had intended to call only the chieftains, but for some reason, every resident had come as well. This was most likely the work of Rick, that fast but careless messenger. Perhaps it was time for Torson to stop sending him on errands. Speed wasn't the only priority when sending a message.

The cramped yard was filled with villagers, their numbers stretching farther than the boundaries of shrubbery. Was it really wise to light a fire with such a crowd congregated around?

While it worried me, it was too late to repel them. I told Torson to keep the spectators away from the pile as best as he could, and he in turn ordered the manor's staff to push people back. The villagers pushed back too, and scuffles started breaking out. There were growls; there were cries. The general atmosphere had become unruly.

How had the simple act of burning trash devolved into this? Had Meg spread her foreboding warning about curses? She was off to one side, observing the proceedings with a grin, though I had no idea what she found so amusing.

Tensions continued to mount, but just before the first serious fistfight broke out, an angry roar reverberated through the air, stopping all in their tracks. The star had finally taken the stage.

Veralgon was being slowly led out of the dragon house. He had already been displeased upon arrival, and now he was far past that stage. It was understandable. He'd been force-fed smithing grass while feeling under the weather, and now, as he was dragged out of the dragon house, he was being swarmed by people without the talent. Of course he'd complain—I would too.

The dragon again roared at the heavens. Screams broke out among the crowd, and even the dragon keeper looked weak in the knees, so I rushed over and took the reins. Veralgon looked at me irately, but it appeared he would comply. As I led him along, the crowd parted at once, clearing a path to the pile.

I sensed Veralgon's wrath grow as he spotted his target. This was bad. I stroked his leg to establish a connection with him. Though such minimal contact could only form an incomplete link, I still detected his intense hatred for the orcish race. By synchronizing his spirit with my own to some extent, I was just barely able to contain his madness.

"Clear a space behind the pile too!"

Hearing my shout, the villagers behind the heap scattered like baby spiders. The dragon was impatient, and he couldn't be held back any longer.

"Do it!"

Veralgon lifted his head, sucked his lungs full of air, then opened his jaws wide as if snapping at prey. Flames sprang from his maw, enveloping the pile of rubbish. In an instant, all of it was turned to a massive pillar of flame, blazing toward the sky. Not a word was uttered by the dazed onlookers as all eyes shone with fire. The former clamoring had been replaced by awed silence, the only sounds coming from the crackling of burning junk and the low murmur of the flames. The fire continued to hold the villagers in a primitive sort of fascination as sparks danced and twirled above them like fairies, floating away into the darkening ceiling of clouds.

Not long after, a droplet struck my face. In looking up, I was pelted by more of them. It was actually a comfortable sensation after my face had been subjected to so much heat. The droplets quickly gained momentum, soon turning into a downpour. Those who stared fixedly into the cold rain seemed shocked out of their daze, raising anxious voices. However, the dragon's flame remained undeterred by the downpour and continued to burn strong.

The shower was over in no time at all. Veralgon spread his wings wide before the mountain of junk, which still burned as brightly as ever. He roared, as if proclaiming his victory over the elements. Inspired, the villagers answered the call, no longer fearing the roars of this mighty creature.

"It's a sacred dragon!" someone cried. "The hero and his sacred dragon have cleared the orcish curse!"

Now a different sort of heat was building. A number of folks had begun dancing around the pyre, their long shadows wavering in the flickering flames. Upon seeing this, more men joined in, grabbing one another by the shoulders and stomping their feet in rhythm. The dancers spun and jumped, creating one strong and steady beat. Their wives sang along to these movements in strange melodies, alien to my ears. I couldn't decipher any of the words, unless they were simply meaningless sounds.

Torson whispered into my ear, "This is a dance for an ancient god. It has been prohibited."

I nodded, but continued watching without a word. Some men, too old to dance, kneeled and prayed to the white dragon. The lord's manor had suddenly become the scene of a festival.

Having let off some steam, Veralgon turned away from the villagers and trudged back toward the dragon house. The dragon keeper hurried after him nervously to take the reins, but by now, Veralgon had calmed down and was docile.

As I watched them depart, I murmured, "Mr. Torson, break open the ale."

Torson headed off to begin ordering the servants. When the barrels were rolled out, the villagers cheered, and so the merry-making continued. At times, young men and women would take each other by the hand and disappear off into the shadows.

The ruckus continued until the pile had burned down to cinders. Wine barrels from the manor's cellar were emptied one after another, and once empty, those barrels were tossed into the pyre to keep the blaze burning. The fire only dwindled once the wine was exhausted, and with the flames, the festive mood subsided. The villagers stared longingly at the dwindling embers before finally returning to their homes.

The impromptu festival was over, leaving behind nothing but ash.

When the site of the pyre at the edge of the estate was eventually exposed to the morning sun, not a flicker of the night's mesmerizing flames remained. There was just a pile of pure-white ash and a hint of black smoke in the air, and the manor's staff moved in to deal with these remnants of the festival. Everyone moved more sluggishly than usual, and there was a peculiar wretchedness hanging in the air after that wild and beautiful night.

As I prepared to mount Veralgon to make for Kerulgarz, Meg came to see me off.

"Should I accompany you? I can make myself useful," she proposed.

Flying with Meg aboard was quite an appealing idea, as I still remembered the sensation from the last time we'd ridden together. However, I needed the dragon keeper this time, since I'd heard there were no keepers stationed at Kerulgarz Castle. It was not impossible for three to ride a dragon, but I couldn't force Veralgon when he was already feeling out of it.

"No need. I just have to see to it that they make peace there is all."

There was no telling what Meg would do if I were to bring her to Kerulgarz. Just yesterday, her rash talk about curses might well have instigated that ruckus. It most likely hadn't been intentional, but she seemed to be a natural trickster. I had the feeling something unexpected would happen whenever I got involved with her, for better or worse. Thus, I thought it unwise to take her to these important peace talks.

"Is that so...?"

Surprisingly, she backed off just like that. *Thank goodness.* She turned to her accompanying butler—or, being a woman, was she still considered a maid, despite her male garments? I supposed it didn't matter.

"Lydia, send a message to my uncle. The retinue may stand down."

"Stand down, you say? Certainly. I will see to it at once."

The woman called Lydia turned to another butler-maid and gave her own order. This servant raced off for the stables and vanished from sight.

"What's this about a retinue?" I asked Meg.

"Nothing. It's just that if we won't be needing my warriors, I thought it best that they return to the castle."

"From where?"

"From the border with Kerulgarz."

Well, that was close. If I'd carelessly taken her up on her offer, she had intended to march her elite warriors into the neighboring territory along with us.

"It is unfortunate that I can't be of any use," she said, her brow creasing sorrowfully. But the way I looked at it, not putting her to use was clearly a blessing.

CHAPTER 2

Cleaning Up After Kerulgarz

While I normally would have headed straight for Kerulgarz, I first wanted to stop by the Hill Temple. Apparently, it was expected that the field marshal would visit the temple upon every trip to Kadann Hill. I honestly wasn't very enthusiastic about it, however, as the rat-faced head priest had managed to wear on my patience something awful the last time I'd been there. There was little to be done about it, though, and thus I had directed Veralgon to fly east. At least this way I could use my mission to Kerulgarz as an excuse to escape any long, droning monologues. I hadn't sent any advance notice either, so if they were too busy to see me, all the better. I was just fulfilling my obligations, for what it's worth.

Knowing that head priest, he no doubt already knew I was back, and he'd likely anticipated my visit as well. That was how it had gone the last time, anyway. In keeping with his seedy looks, he was the sort of man I had to keep an eye on.

When Veralgon had descended near the temple entrance, the rat-faced man came scampering out in a panic. His face was pale, a waterfall of sweat flowing from his brow. This was not the reaction I'd been expecting, and I wondered why he was in this state. Once I'd jumped down, the head priest approached me, his hands groping at the air.

"Wh-why, if it isn't our esteemed field marshal," he stammered. "I've heard great things about your accomplishments. Indeed, rumor has it you led your dragon to deliver divine judgment unto countless orcs. I'm sure God is delighted by your work. In any case, what brings you here on this fine day?"

The priest glanced anxiously at the white dragon behind me. Veralgon was in a bad mood—which was hardly anything new. He had somewhat calmed down during the festivities, but he still exuded a discontented energy. Perhaps I'd done something I shouldn't have. At times like this, even the dragon keepers were spooked by him.

"I apologize for dropping by without prior notice," I said. "It's nothing important. As I've just returned to the territory, I simply wanted to pay my respects."

"How courteous of you. Many thanks—much appreciated. Why don't we have a nice chat inside the temple? I don't have much to offer, but please feel right at home." Even as he said this, it was quite clear the head priest didn't want me to stay long. Nor did I want to, so at least we shared a common goal.

"To tell you the truth, I have a mission ahead of me from His Majesty himself. You'll have to pardon the brevity of my visit."

"Oh, is that so? What a shame," he said, looking terribly relieved. To be fair, not many people could keep their cool around such a dangerous dragon.

With a bow to the priest, I turned to hop aboard Veralgon again. The dragon broke into a gallop, increasing speed while spreading his massive wings, and once he had gained enough speed, we shot upward with a mighty flap. With each beat of his wings, we rose higher.

This time our course was south, toward our destination: Kerulgarz Castle.

From a distance, Kerulgarz Castle gave the appearance of having emerged directly from a lake. My best guess was that it had actually been built on the lake's edge, but vast moats had been dug all around the building, making it appear as if the castle floated on the water's surface. The northern face—the one facing the lake—had no protective walls, instead opting for a dock that jutted out into the water. The land side, however, was fortified by a massive gate.

I circled Veralgon overhead, using roars to send signals below. As Rigel had instructed me beforehand, I dropped altitude over the lake and landed on the dock.

In the forecourt, the master and his vassals had already formed an orderly line to welcome me. Judging from their attire, the one standing in the center, a step ahead of the rest, was the master of the castle and hence the lord of Kerulgarz. The others behind him were obviously his lesser lords.

I was surprised to find I actually recognized the lord. He explained, "The baton was passed from my father to my brother, and then to me. My name is Thret. It has been a while, Hero."

Thret had been one of the survivors of the great battle. We'd both been tasked with reporting the aftermath of the battle to His Majesty. I'd heard he was a youth of prestigious lineage, but I never thought I'd meet him here.

I learned bits and pieces of his story as we walked together. After the reporting ceremony, he'd returned home for his father's funeral. However, word of his father's death had caused his sickly elder brother's health to take a bad turn, and he'd followed close behind. At the loss of its lord and his eldest son, Kerulgarz had quickly fallen into chaos. As the oldest remaining heir, Thret was hoisted up as the next leader before he knew it.

That was all well and good. However, as luck would have it, his mother was merely a lowly knight's daughter. Meanwhile, his youngest brother had been born to the daughter of a lesser lord of prominent standing. The latter's house protested Thret's new position, claiming Thret's lineage made him unfit and insisting that their child should be the one to take the seat. They rallied the other lesser lords and their armies. Meanwhile, a third group had taken advantage of the mess in an effort to prop up another younger brother. Just like that, Kerulgarz had fallen into a three-way civil war. Recently, Thret had finally managed to defeat the rebels.

"Thank you for coming all the way out here. I apologize for the trouble I caused while I fumbled with the situation."

"Don't worry about it. It's all part of the job."

He was apologizing, yet he'd managed to resolve a civil war in just a month. He was just as proficient as I would expect from someone who had survived that battle.

Thret led me into a massive hall, where two rows of long tables faced each other. Half of the seats—those closest to the door—were already occupied. The moment we entered, everyone immediately rose and stood at attention. Many of these individuals wore clothing covered in mud, and some leaked blood from where the material was ripped. Some even had their heads wrapped in pus-stained bandages. It soon dawned on me that everyone in this room had been on the losing side of the civil war. They had presumably been taken as prisoners of war.

With Thret leading me, I walked between the rows of tables to the seat farthest in the back. The place of honor, so to speak. The lesser lords took the long way around, taking their positions at the heads of the tables. There, they stood at attention just like the others.

Thret made sure everyone was in position, then introduced me. "This is the field marshal upon whom His Majesty has bestowed full control of the military—as well the messenger God has sent from another world! He has come today to oversee peace talks in the name of His Majesty, and to serve as our witness!"

Everyone apart from Thret drew their swords and held them out with the tips pointed down, then bowed to me. *What am I supposed to do at a time like this? Right, something about drawing my sword.*

I drew my blade and brandished it high, overlooking everyone in the hall. Then I clicked it firmly back into its sheath, and the rest tucked their swords away again. It seemed I'd followed through correctly, and I sent a silent thank-you out to my etiquette instructor. When I took my seat, everyone else followed suit. Meanwhile, Thret signaled to an attendant, who came over to him with a large roll of parchment in his hands.

"We will now review the terms of our peace treaty. Anyone who has an objection is free to raise it," Thret said, looking the lords over. "If you will."

"Yes, sir!"

The attendant unfurled the parchment and read each condition in turn. "Firstly, everyone in attendance agrees to recognize Thret, son of Worgan, as the lord of Kerulgarz. Secondly, all lords subject to Kerulgarz shall swear loyalty to Thret. Thirdly..."

The provisions covered all sorts of items from altering borders to ransoms and reparations, to the retirement of active lords, the appointment of their successors, and the promises of marriage between them. The losers listened with bitter expressions, but not one of them voiced dissent. The war was already settled.

Once the last condition had been read aloud, Thret stood and drew his sword. "This is your last chance to speak out! Come forth if you wish to oppose this treaty! You need only best me by the blade!"

Of course, no one said a thing.

"Then we have reached a consensus. Now for the ceremony of vows!"

He gestured for me to follow, and then headed for the exit with the lesser lords trailing behind us. We made our way to a corner of the yard.

Here were seven standing stones, each about human height and covered in moss. It looked as if they'd been plucked right from their homes and put on display. These upright stones formed a circle around an area of ground elevated like a sumo ring, a flat horizontal stone positioned at its center. Thret stood before the central stone and looked up at the sky. The sun had just reached its zenith, its winter rays casting slivers of shadow behind the megaliths.

"Perfect timing. Now offer your vows."

Apparently, it was their tradition to offer their vows of loyalty within this stone circle when the sun was at its strongest. The lesser lords kneeled before Thret one by one, placing a hand on the central stone and speaking their oaths. It wasn't long before everyone had said their vows, and Thret nodded in satisfaction.

"The vows have been made with God, the sun, and God's chosen hero as our witness. You would do well to honor them!"

The lords bowed their heads again, and then the ceremony was complete. With the war officially ended, an air of relief came over the scene. I had now been released from my duties. When I glanced over at Thret, however, I detected an unpleasant nervousness flickering across his face. Was there still something else? But the expression was gone in an instant, and he went on as if nothing were amiss.

"Next, we will commence with the execution of the traitors! Bring them forth!"

The air once again became tense. I understood then that even if not every one of the conquered enemies was to be put to death, they still needed to execute a few of them to hammer their point home. Or perhaps these few had earned themselves an extra level of resentment for their actions during the intense clashes.

On Thret's orders, a number of prisoners were dragged to the altar stone from the underground dungeons. The expressions of the vanquished lords immediately turned grave, while those of the victors were varied. The ones who looked satisfied were no doubt glad they had joined the winning side, whereas those off to one side looking awkward had presumably switched loyalties late in the game. While a minority, a few others even looked sympathetic. However, their eyes were not directed at the prisoners—strangely enough, they were looking straight at Thret.

I soon realized why. A six-year-old child walked to the head of the death row procession. He was, most likely, Thret's younger brother.

Thret, son of Lord Worgan of Kerulgarz, had returned to his homeland after the reporting ceremony to mourn the loss of his father. Worgan had been a good father to him, but he found he wasn't too sorrowful that the man had died. Rather, he believed his father had found a perfect place to die. Shoulder to shoulder with the Princess Knight and the Lion of Morsharz, he had fallen only after fighting to the bitter friend. A warrior to the core, his father had always imagined this end for himself.

Thret didn't have any worries about what was to come next. Worgan had often told others what he wanted to transpire upon his death. Fighter that he was, constantly dancing with death, Worgan had always known that certain decisions had to be made.

According to Worgan, his eldest son, Worren, would become the next head of the house. His second son, Thret, would be Worren's knight, and the third son, Gils, would become a priest. The younger two were expected to support Worren utterly. Worgan hadn't yet prepared an appropriate position for the fourth son, Harlest, to assume one day, but he'd taught the boy to do his best to support his eldest brother. The reason his will was more ambiguous when it came to Harlest was because the boy was only six years old at the time, so naturally, he didn't know what he wanted to do with his life.

Thret had no objections to the will. Contrary to popular opinion, Worgan's sons shared quite a favorable relationship. The eldest brother was sickly, but no one could find fault with his nature and intellect. Thret would become his brother's sword in leading the troops. Gils had the highest capacity for magic, and he would unite the temples in the territory, thus reassuring the populace. Still, what would the youngest brother do?

He was a bright boy, so what about sending him to the palace to learn how to mediate matters with the higher-ups? Worren would surely find the perfect role for him sooner or later. In any case, Thret at least knew what he had to do. He had sustained heavy injuries in the battle, but he knew he and his brothers would be able to overcome them together. That was the future Thret saw laid out before him.

And so, he accepted his father's death, but his brother's death was a different matter entirely.

The night of their father's funeral, when Thret learned of his brother's worsening condition, he turned white as a sheet. Thret had received a knight's education and had done his best to stay well away from politics, but he knew enough to understand the weight of these circumstances. His brother was at the center of his siblings' future, so it was clear what would happen if he died.

Thret's frantic efforts to treat Worren were in vain, and he drew his last breath the next day.

There was no time to wallow in grief. Upon his brother's death, Thret immediately set to action. He needed to hurry to secure his brothers' support, but he was already too late. Before Worren had even gone cold, the two youngest brothers were whisked away to their respective mothers' houses. The reason was clear. Both grandfathers were plotting to install their respective grandsons as the next head of the house instead of Thret.

On his maternal side, Thret hailed from the house of a lowly knight. With this house providing no backing whatsoever, the other families considered him a minor obstacle to overcome. Even so, if a little politicking was all it took for one of his younger brothers to become lord in his place, Thret would have been fine with serving them. A slight change of plans, that was all.

However, unpleasant rumors soon began spreading. These rumors claimed that Thret had poisoned his older brother. He never learned who had started them, but they were a clear declaration of war. His enemy didn't intend to leave any room for Thret in their vision for the future. They planned on branding him a traitor in order to remove him completely.

His late father, Worren, had been a proud knight, and Thret took after him more than any of his brothers did. *Very well,* he thought. *If you want to pick a fight, you'll get one.*

A knight never turned down a challenge, so Thret resolved himself. He had very few allies, but neither did he stand alone, so he felt he had a chance.

He went on to win the war.

The prisoners formed a line before the stone circle. The child farthest to the right was brought out to the front. He seemed fearful, though he didn't shed a tear. No doubt this was what was expected of a great lord's son, and I was impressed. How would I have fared at his age? I'd been quite the brat, so if I had been in his shoes, I was sure I would have been bawling my eyes out, rolling and kicking on the ground.

A bearded man behind Thret whispered something in his ear. The lord silently shook his head, and the man backed off. Then, Thret drew his sword and assumed a stance, his face expressionless.

The onlookers waited for what was to come, all eyes gathered on the two brothers in the center of the stone circle. With his overseers thus distracted, an elderly man escaped from the line and leapt forward, hands still bound. He was quickly seized and thrown to the ground, but even then, he attempted to crawl to Thret.

"Lord Thret! Lord of Kerulgarz! Our merciful lord!" he pleaded. "Harlest is innocent! We propped him up and put words in his mouth! The responsibility lies with me! Please, I beg you, spare my grandson—spare your brother!"

Here was the ringleader, an influential lesser lord who had put his grandson on a pedestal and raised a flag of rebellion. Everyone returned their gaze to Thret, wondering how he would react.

"Silence, impudent fool!" Thret exploded, then launched a powerful kick into the face of the man who groveled at his feet. "Do you think that will work on me, after all you've done? If you had won, did you have any intention of sparing my life?"

Thret's face conveyed a terrible mix of sorrow and wrath.

"O-of course, I—"

"Why did you raise an army without one word to me? Why spread vile rumors that I'd poisoned Worren?!"

Just as the prisoner opened his mouth to justify himself, Thret kicked him in the stomach, causing him to choke. Still, he continued to speak through all his coughing.

"Y-Your Excellency... Please... Sh-show mercy. Your hands must not be sullied with the blood of your own. This is the final advice from someone bound for the grave..."

"As if you have any right to advise me! Whose fault do you think all this is?"

Smacked by the flat of Thret's sword, the old man's jaw shattered. Now he could no longer protest nor even make meaningful sounds.

"This one hangs. He doesn't deserve the Garden of Warriors."

Thret pointed toward the stables, and the prisoner's face went pale. The castle servants scrambled into action, swiftly preparing a platform of wood and lashing a rope to the stable's eaves. When the impromptu gallows was ready, soldiers dragged the struggling old man toward it.

"No, not yet." Thret's voice was cold as ice, and he looked to the skies for a moment. "He must first witness the conclusion of what he's wrought."

By the time Thret's eyes returned to his young brother, he had stifled his emotions once more. "It's time," he said softly, holding his sword aloft.

Harlest looked him in the eye. "I won't resent you," he said. With that, he bowed his head, presenting his neck. The six-year-old was surely trying to be as dignified as he could, and considerate toward his older brother.

How foolish, I thought. *It's going to have the opposite effect.*

Thret was frozen now, tears in his eyes.

In the corner of my eye, I could see the bearded man from before approaching Thret with a hand on his hilt. There was no way around it; I would have to play the villain. I extended a spear of light to keep the bearded man where he was. He looked at me as though he wanted to say something, but I shook my head and urged him to stand down. Then I turned to Thret.

"Sir... You're keeping them waiting."

Thret could have left this to his court executioner from the start, but now that he had already drawn his own sword, he could no longer back down from his duty. He glared at me through teary eyes. *I know,* his expression seemed to say. Then he dropped his gaze and took the swing. It was a clean cut. With a powerful slash like that, he wouldn't have given his little brother a second in which to feel pain.

The rest of the prisoners were then dragged before Thret in turn and executed without further incident. Meanwhile, a single body swayed from the eaves of the nearby stables.

The bloodstained ceremony transitioned into a banquet. A fire was lit in the center of the castle's grand hall, and a large cow was roasted whole upon it. Chicken, pork, venison, and wild boar dishes covered the tables, which were arranged in a circle around the fire, and there were heaps of apples, grapes, and some fruits I'd never seen before. There weren't any chairs, and the feast was held buffet style.

Wine barrels filled the spaces between the tables, around which gathered the lesser lords and their attending subjects. All the feast's participants seemed overtaken with the urge to drink themselves out of their minds.

Thret stood before the flames, a drinking horn in hand, and spoke some opening words.

"Gentlemen... The battle is over! We've all shed blood, and many courageous warriors have fallen, but now we move forward. Meager as it is, I've modeled this banquet after the feasts in the Garden of Warriors. In that garden, we are not divided into friend and foe. It is said that there, fallen warriors laud each other's exploits while enjoying endless feasts."

I figured the Garden of Warriors he referred to was something akin to Valhalla.

"Tonight, think of this hall as the realm of the dead! Wash the grudges away with ale, and pray they don't follow you back to the mortal plane. We are whole once more!"

Thret raised his drinking vessel. The men gathered in the hall cried out with throaty voices, holding their own horns high. Boisterous as it was, the banquet carried on peacefully.

Beside me, a man who had lost everything below the wrist on one arm showed off his wound and proclaimed, "Have a look at this wound! I earned it when I bested Marold the Brave!"

"Marold was my uncle," a young knight called back. "One-eyed Marold. So you're the one who got him."

"Indeed, and he was truly formidable. You should be proud to share blood with a warrior so noble."

The one-handed man gave the young knight a pat on the back. They then exchanged horns and drained each other's. Those who had been fighting only days earlier now spoke glowingly of the exploits of enemies, bragged about their own wounds, and shared a laugh. I heard raucous singing burst out here and there—all war songs. I had witnessed this very same scene in a number of worlds.

Apparently, it hadn't been all that rare in my own world, if one went back far enough. There was a time when I wouldn't have been able to comprehend how men could reconcile like this, cheering about their wounds as if it were sport. Did wars drive men mad and skew their perspectives?

I didn't think so. After throwing myself into a number of battles as their hero, I had begun to understand where they were coming from. This banquet was a necessity, a ceremony that allowed them to reassert their humanity.

All humans liked to believe that they could love and respect others. That was their instinct as social animals. However, that ideal would fall to pieces once a human faced a hostile enemy on the battlefield. This hostility overpowered one's better nature and left deep scars on the spirit. No matter how much a person loved their allies, they couldn't counterbalance the power of hatred and malice. These challenges threatened their self-esteem and scorched their soul.

What if the hostility between humans was solely a result of a difference in social standing? What if that malice wasn't directed at the *individual*, but a system? And then, what would happen once standings were equalized and the war was over?

This banquet was a setting where they could learn those things. There were wounds only former enemies could heal. Reconciliation was a form of therapy for each of them.

Of course, human emotion was too complex for everyone to react the same way. There were those in the corners who kept to themselves and their friends. There were those who tactfully, or sometimes brazenly, avoided those who had done them wrong. It was impossible for the ale to wash all the grudges away, but for the time being, Thret would need to let their relationships play out.

This space for reconciliation could only be formed by warriors who had opposed each other on equal ground. Those subjected to unfair, one-sided aggression would never be able to join cups in forgiveness. For instance, if the court had invited citizens from burned villages to this banquet, the proceedings would have turned murderous.

As things stood now, with the price of food rising due to a terrible harvest, the lord would need to take the utmost care in placating his subjects. It was not an enviable position to be in.

I scanned the hall to see what that selfsame lord had gotten up to. I spotted him right as he was taking his leave. Beside him was with the bearded man from earlier in the day—likely a close associate. Thret's wounds were of a sort this banquet could not heal. I thought that perhaps I should go talk with him and let him vent his feelings. I didn't want someone as capable as him to falter and fail as a result of what he'd had to do.

I roughly parted the seas of drunks and made for the door. I myself was drunk enough to act out of character.

Though I had followed Thret out of the hall, by the time I reached the corridor beyond, he was no longer in sight. From a passing servant, I learned the lord would likely be found in his private chamber, which was on the floor above.

There, I found the man with the beard blocking the closed door. Did he always accompany Thret? They seemed quite close, both personally and professionally. When he noticed a figure approaching, he immediately braced for trouble, but he backed off with a bow once he recognized it was me. His beard gave him an air of maturity, but up close, I saw that he was surprisingly young—perhaps only in his late twenties, like Thret and myself.

"My lord is resting within. Please wait," the man said, then he let himself into the room. He returned almost immediately. "Please follow me."

The bearded man lowered his head deferentially and ushered me inside. Our eyes met as I passed him, and there was a peculiar, conflicted light in his gaze. I couldn't know exactly how he felt about me, but he was certainly wary, or at least worried. After all, I was the one who had directed him to hold back, thereby forcing Thret to personally cut down his own little brother. Was he concerned that I would agitate his heartbroken lord again?

The new lord welcomed me with a drained smile on his face.

"Thank you for what you did back there," he said, motioning for me to sit. He was likely talking about the execution.

"I hope I didn't step out of line."

"No, you saved me. If you hadn't stopped Ricard, he would have taken over my role as executioner."

If Thret were to be seen as a leader whose emotions prevented him from personally dealing with an outlaw, his subordinates would lose respect for him. He seemed to be well aware of this, so I seriously doubted I had earned his resentment, though of course, I couldn't know what was going on in his head.

"So, Hero, did you need something from me?"

"No, nothing. I simply saw that you were feeling down, so I thought we might have a little chat."

"I...appreciate your consideration."

A prolonged silence settled between us. Alcohol had done wonders carrying me all the way to his room, but now that I was here, I realized I actually knew very little about him, especially in regard to how to cheer him up. As the awkwardness dragged on, the only solution I could come up with was a little reminiscing about myself.

"Some time ago, one of my comrades was forced to kill his own daughter. She was around the same age as Harlest. She was adorable and kind."

"Why did it come to that?"

"It was my fault."

I wasn't going to make any excuses. I had underestimated the amount of mana needed for a crucial ritual, so a sacrifice had been required to cover the deficit. It had become a necessity—there was no time for an alternative. That child was the only other one there, aside from those who were necessary to complete the rite.

"I won't go into the details, but my mistake meant a sacrifice was necessary."

It would have taken too much time to explain how magic worked in that other world, and even if I had done so, it would only have sounded like a pathetic attempt to justify myself.

"Anyway, this man weighed his duties against his daughter, and he decided to end her life by his own hand."

With seconds to spare, my comrade had killed the girl without even being able to tell her goodbye. She'd cried as she met her end.

"What happened next?" Thret asked, leaning toward me.

"After his daughter's death, the man was overcome with grief... but the world avoided total annihilation."

"And then? How did that man get back on his feet?"

"He never did. He was still grieving when he lost his life during the next battle. Right to the end, he never made peace with himself."

Thret hung his head and fell silent. I could never forget that haunting event, yet I always feared remembering it. I now regretted having related it to Thret, however, as there was no hope to be found in that story, so I tried another one.

"I once had to cut down a father before his son's eyes."

Yet another story I didn't want to remember, but felt compelled to express.

"The man had betrayed us, leaking information to the enemy. His son understood the crime but told me he couldn't take the life of his own father, his last living blood...so he handed his sword to me."

Thret lifted his head, looking at me with dark eyes. "What happened then?"

"He resented me thereafter, and no doubt still does."

Given his father's deeds, it was unreasonable that the boy should direct his anger at me, but the human heart was never reasonable to begin with.

"Looks like things never go as we want them to," Threet sighed, again hanging his head. I had clearly failed in putting his act into perspective, and in fact had only made matters worse.

The silence resumed. At this point, I just wanted to get up and leave, but it didn't seem right to leave him in this state. It was better that I tried to get him to do the talking. *I remember a doctor once telling me that listening is the essence of counseling.*

"Can you tell me more about your family?"

Threet looked up, then back down. "I don't have a family anymore. My mother died shortly after having me. My father perished in the last war. My brothers..."

He wouldn't go on from there, as if he'd strayed over a landmine. No, that wasn't the right word for bombs that lay in the open for everyone to see.

With the silence refusing to be dispelled, I was again wondering how I might gracefully escape, when Threet suddenly started talking again.

"Well, at least I still have Ricard."

"Do you mean that man outside the door?"

"Yes. He heads my retinue."

Why did he speak of Ricard as family? They didn't appear to be linked by blood. Was it an intimate relationship? Those practices came about easily among warriors—young men with only one another for close company for days, months, even years at a stretch.

"Ricard is my milk brother."

Ah, now I understood. With his own mother dead, Ricard's mother had been Thret's wet nurse. The two boys had both been nourished at the same breast.

"We've practically been brothers from birth. When I resolved to fight the rebels, Ricard stood with me." With a sad smile, he went on, "It was his grandfather who led the rebellion. Ricard was Harlest's cousin, you see. He could have joined their side, but he rejected his family to follow me. It is thanks to him that I won."

"You were blessed to have such a fine vassal."

"Yes, my thoughts exactly. I've seen so many traitors and turncoats in this war. By now, he's the only one I can trust in the truest sense." Thret heaved a deep sigh. "I envy you, Hero."

"How so?"

"You're not tied to blood or land here. You're free."

So that was how it looked to him. "I am free in that sense, I suppose, because I have nothing. Wandering from world to world, how could I ever keep a single friend?"

I was actually envious of Thret. He had a trustworthy comrade, and a home to protect. I myself had neither. Of course, if I spent enough years in a single world, I could find a comrade and a home—but only until that world was saved. When this was accomplished, I would be sent back to my original world, and all that I'd gained would be gone. Such things could only ever be temporary for me. Even in my original world, everything served as short, fleeting interludes between voyages. My old friends had already moved on in their lives without me.

"Things never really go our way, do they?" Thret muttered.

"Not really."

Silence again. While it might have been my imagination, this silence was not as heavy as before. I had the feeling that the conversation had reached a comfortable-enough conclusion, but as I rose to leave, Thret spoke once more.

"Hero, I must once again express my gratitude to you."

I didn't think I'd done anything worth his thanks. "For what?"

"For stopping Ricard. If I had let Ricard cut the condemned down, then like the man in that story of yours, perhaps I would have resented the only family I had left."

Perhaps so, and that reaction would have felt unreasonable to Ricard, but the human heart was an irrational thing.

"I think you should go have a long chat with someone who knew Harlest well. Perhaps Ricard himself fits the bill. It's the least you can do to see off the dead."

"Yes. I'll try."

At last, the time had finally come to depart. I bowed to Thret, and when I returned to the corridor, Ricard bowed deeply to me. I tried returning the gesture, but his head didn't rise, so I left him that way. Behind me, I heard the sound of a door opening, then faint voices from within the room. By the time I glanced back, the door had already closed and Ricard was gone.

I didn't feel any inclination to return to the banquet and instead retired to the guest room provided for me. While I sat there, gazing off into space, I received a midnight visitor. I opened the door to find Ricard standing there.

"Allow me to thank you for what you did before. Meeting you has allowed my lord to process his emotions."

This man truly was the loyal sort, to seek me out and say that. I could understand why Thret trusted him.

"I didn't do much. It's you who has greatly supported Thret."

Ricard smiled at that, but I could tell he had more he wanted to say.

"Is there something else on your mind?"

"There is one thing I want to ask of you, Hero."

"I'll do whatever's within my capabilities."

After hesitating for a moment, Ricard got into it. "Truth be told, there is one person left who should have received judgment for the civil war."

Ah, just as I'd thought; this had been bothering me as well. Thret had two younger brothers, and different factions had tried to install both of them as lords, yet so far, only the youngest had been apprehended and executed. I'd figured that the other had died on the battlefield, but perhaps not.

"Gils, the remaining brother, has evaded our pursuit and is still on the run."

"Does he pose a threat?"

Gils had likely only been a figurehead, but based on his status, might he still be capable of reigniting the rebellion? Could the war truly be considered over, with someone like that prowling around behind the scenes?

"All his prominent backers have either died or sworn allegiance to Thret. There shouldn't be any problems there."

"Then what do you want me for?"

"After tracing his trail, we've determined there's a strong likelihood he fled to the neighboring territory."

"Oh?" I had a bad feeling about that.

"Yes. To Kadann Hill."

To my territory, then.

"Do you seek my permission to search there?"

Kadann Hill was under my management, but the actual owner of the land was His Majesty the King, so I wasn't sure if I had the authority to give such permission.

"No, not exactly. We have a pretty good idea of where he is. Gils has a relative there."

A relative in my territory? Were they related to Thret too? I couldn't think of who this person might be, and where they would be hiding him...until a thought occurred to me.

"Someone at the Hill Temple?"

"Indeed." Ricard gave a solemn nod. "The head priest is Gils's uncle on his mother's side."

I recalled how hard the rat-faced head priest had pushed the third son the first time we'd met, and how panicked he'd been when I'd stopped in at the temple that morning. When he'd learned I was on my way to help stabilize Kerulgarz, he must have misunderstood that I was at the Hill Temple to capture his fugitive nephew.

"I see. Upon my return journey home, I'll negotiate with the temple to secure Gils. Should I then hand him over to Thret?"

"No, there is no need. As I've said, he no longer has any backing." His answer caught me a little off guard. Ricard lowered his voice, as if some eavesdropper might be listening. "You need only pass on this message. Tell Gils he must never return to Kerulgarz."

"I'll do that. But does Thret know about any of this?"

"I am acting of my own discretion."

I looked him straight in the eyes, and he didn't look away. Good—his were not the eyes of a traitor. Presumably, he didn't want to place any more burden on Thret than the man was already dealing with. I respected Ricard for being so protective of his lord, though it was a bit much.

"Understood. A message it is, then. To anyone else, I know nothing about Gils's whereabouts, and I haven't heard anything from you regarding him. Does that sound satisfactory?" Anything beyond that was his to deal with; I sure wasn't planning on taking charge of the situation.

"It does, sir. Thank you."

I asked Ricard for some bits of information I could use to confirm Gils's identity. Having provided these, he gave me a knightly salute and then took his leave.

After I'd seen him off, I felt a touch of regret. Delivering the message would mean I would have to see that unpleasant rat-faced priest again. It was almost enough to make me wish I hadn't given my word.

Once I'd returned to my territory of Kadann Hill, I immediately headed for the Hill Temple. I left Veralgon far enough away that he wouldn't be intimidating and soothed him as I directed him to wait. The dragon keeper was reluctant to be left alone with the vicious dragon, but I just couldn't allow Veralgon to frighten the pitiful head priest this time. Fortunately, since the bonfire festival the day before yesterday, Veralgon had regained a more even temperament. The dragon keeper would probably have no difficulties.

Even before I'd learned he was sheltering an outlaw, the head priest of the Hill Temple had given me the same vibes as some petty villain. However, while my first impression of him hadn't been the greatest, I could understand his actions given the circumstances. The man must have been desperate to help his nephew, whose faction had been in the worst situation among the three warring forces. So this was why he had approached me in the past with such biased information, in an attempt to get me to join the civil war.

In fact, the man would have handled the subterfuge better if he really was the schemer type. Deep down, he was probably an honest man, as one would expect of the head priest of a sacred land. I recalled how he'd lamented the losses of the farmers when he'd ranted to me about the war. No doubt, these had been his sincere emotions.

Undoubtedly, Thret was merciless in war. I was sure he wouldn't have hesitated to set fires and plunder to achieve victory. Merciless or not, his tactics were incredibly effective. On the way to Kerulgarz and back, I'd spotted a number of settlements that had been burnt to the ground.

After having reconsidered my view of the head priest, it felt less burdensome meeting with him. Of course, I didn't expect him to readily admit to sheltering Gils. I was certain he would use every means at his disposal to keep his precious nephew hidden away. Still, no matter how he might deny or protest, I would still pass along the message to him. Given that Ricard didn't intend to have Gils brought back for punishment, the contents of the message should actually come as good news.

Of course, I didn't know how the message might really be received. Perhaps Gils would feel compelled to return to Kerulgarz even if it meant his death. I wouldn't interfere whichever way it went. If Gils preferred to cast away his past and live in my territory, I would gladly play the fool. Even if Thret were to come around with questions, I would feign ignorance, just as I had promised Ricard.

The head priest of the Hill Temple had likely spotted the flying dragon in the distance. No sooner had I appeared at the temple than the head priest came out to meet me. In his hand, he held the end of a chain that was tightly wound around a battered and bruised young man—a young man who bore a strong resemblance to Thret, minus the warrior's glint in the older brother's eyes.

Having reached me, the head priest fell prostrate, his words coming at machine-gun speed.

"Oh! If it isn't our merciful Hero, handpicked by God Himself! First, I must inform you that I have absolutely no intention of rebellion. You need to be aware of that! I never planned on sheltering a rebel! I simply never noticed that this filthy rat had snuck his way onto our sacred grounds! Here! You see? As evidence, I have captured the rebel myself!"

What was going on here?

Gils cried, "Uncle, what is the meaning of this? Didn't you say you'd ensure my—"

"Silence, rebel! How brazen could you be, fleeing into a holy temple after rejecting God's will? A shameful little rat like you would be better suited to trembling in a rotted tree hollow!"

This was not at all what I'd expected. I'd intended to impart Ricard's words to the priest, then make my exit while he gushed his thanks behind me.

As I stood there confused, the head priest kicked Gils in the back. The young man toppled at my feet. Still bound with chain, he struggled upright to rest on his knees, looking up at me. His expression already looked resolved.

"I'll deal with him myself, Hero!" the priest said, already raising a hatchet above his head. Gils glared at him but didn't resist.

"Wait, wait, wait!" I stepped in to hold the priest back. "I didn't come here to capture him."

"Huh?"

"Sir Ricard gave me a secret message to pass on to you. He said that so long as Gils agrees to never return to Kerulgarz, and so long as he discards his past and repents, he will turn a blind eye."

Uncle and nephew shared a perplexed look.

"Who is this fellow, anyway?" I asked. "I didn't hear anything about there being a fugitive here."

Finally coming to his senses, dripping with cold sweat, the head priest lowered his hatchet.

"Th-that's right, that's right! This boy's an assistant we keep around the temple! He has a habit of taking things that aren't his, and he frequently sticks his hands into our food storage, so I was disciplining him! You couldn't have come at a worse time, Hero! You've witnessed something truly unsightly. Oh, how embarrassing! Come now, boy! Repent, you gluttonous rat!"

The head priest began kicking Gils, who had been demoted from a refugee vying for a throne to a sticky-fingered hungry brat.

The young man glared back scornfully. "Uncle! After you included me in your plot to overthrow the government, this is how you treat me?"

"Wh-wh...what are you saying? Enough of this nonsense! Hero, listen to me! I don't know what he's talking about! This child tends to conflate delusions with reality..."

Gils thrust out his neck and cried, "Hero, I've already resolved myself to my punishment! Cut me down now, and present my head to my brother! He will face many troubles if my fate is left uncertain!"

Give me a break. Why do I have to do the dirty work?

"Calm down, both of you. I'll take him with me; how does that sound?"

Gils obviously couldn't remain here anymore, after his craven uncle's betrayal. There wasn't much else I could do, so I decided I'd leave him with Torson and put him to work in my territory. No doubt, Torson would appreciate having another helper.

Yet the rat-priest expressed disapproval at this proposal. "O-oh... What compassion. But Hero, he is a terrible kleptomaniac. He cannot help it! He is not worthy of working under you."

"I trust Torson to train him well."

"A-and also... That's right! Did I tell you he is a habitual liar? Yes, he lies just as easily as he breathes! Can't trust a word he says! A real snake in the grass!"

The priest was sweating profusely. He must've feared what might happen if I took the young man with me. After all, from what Gils had told me, the head priest was one of the ring-leaders who'd sparked civil war in Kerulgarz. He'd obviously intended to increase his own influence by having a relative in a high position. If Gils's testimony managed to incriminate him, at minimum, he would be in quite a precarious situation. As long as I had Gils, I'd have the priest gripped by the scruff of his neck.

"I actually think he looks to be a clever sort. I'll take him; don't you worry about it."

"He is a heinous criminal who has stolen the property of a sacred temple! His deeds warrant death!"

"Even more reason not to leave him here. Rather than have him die in a ditch, I'd prefer to put his intellect to good use."

I manifested a spear of light and stroked it against the prisoner's chains. Upon seeing the metal links part and fall away so easily, the priest turned pale, yet he still ran his mouth.

"Hero, I heard rumor of a peculiar ceremony carried out at your residence the other day. Now you come to my temple to steal a sinner. Why, this is blasphemy, pagan worship, and disrespect of sacred ground! These are grounds for excommunication."

I was surprised he'd managed to say all this through his quivering. His courage deserved a modicum of respect. It seemed he wasn't a complete worm.

"Well, you'll have to bring those charges to the capital and explain them to His Majesty and his ministers. Of course, when that happens, I'm sure this boy will confess everything he knows before God."

The ceremony he'd spoken of had simply been a trash fire. However, if I couldn't avoid excommunication, it honestly didn't mean much to me. The temple was a powerful backer, but I had other allies, such as the dragon riders. The Knights Templar were in the middle of a reorganization, and they were not part of my forces. Anyway, excommunicating God's messenger was quite a notion. What would this priest get in exchange? A scandal like that would just give his political enemies more ammunition to use against him.

Seeing the head priest's features contort in irritation, I knew I had hit the mark.

"Hero, may I ask something, then?"

"What is it?"

"What precisely do you intend to do with a fugitive from Kerulgarz?"

"Nothing much. I thought he could help out with finances, perhaps."

Thret was a war buddy who had survived the battlefield with me. I had no intention of stirring up his life any further.

That wasn't to say I didn't have any ulterior motives—for instance, using Gils's safety as an incentive to get him to join the fight against the orcs once more. Still, in the end, I would respect Gils's wishes regarding his fate. If he wanted to return home, no matter what the consequences might be, then send him to Ricard I would.

I returned to the manor with Gils on foot. The dragon keeper kept Veralgon on a lead a short distance away, since the dragon would try to bite Gils if he got too close. Gils didn't have the talent, and it seemed he couldn't ride. Even if that hadn't been the case, I didn't want to load the dragon with three riders. I'd considered flying back on my own to fetch a horse, but that idea made me anxious. The head priest could try to silence Gils in my absence.

I asked the young man some questions as we walked.

"You'll be in my care for the time being. Are you all right with that?"

"Yes."

Naturally, Gils was completely grief-stricken after all that had occurred.

"We'll need to think up a new name for you. Any suggestions?"

"No, not particularly."

"Then George it is."

"Very well."

He was like this all the way to our destination...not that I blamed him.

"I don't mind if you remain in your room for a time until you feel more at ease, but that might get pretty boring. I'd like to send some jobs your way. Any requests?"

"No, not particularly."

"Can you read? Write? How are you at math?"

"I have received a basic temple education."

"I see. What other things did they teach you there?"

"They taught me God's teachings. I know blessings and prayers. I also know war ceremonies, but I can't draw magic circles."

Among the war ceremonies was a spell that provided a protective barrier. By sending mana into a circle traced upon the ground, a normal shield fitted with an appropriate talisman could exhibit effects on par with a shield of light. However, I could already produce protective shields at will. Also, we already had more than enough priests in our territory, so how would I make use of him?

"What job were you originally aiming for in your own territory?"

Gils—or, rather, George—looked terribly sad at this question. His future had just been thrown into chaos, and here I was asking him about a former future he had envisioned for himself. I regretted asking the question.

Nevertheless, he answered. "After receiving my vestments, I would have been sent to some distant temple to gain practical experience. Then, after training further at the capital's grand temple and advancing my rank, I would have returned to Kerulgarz as the castle's personal priest, to support my father and brother."

According to George, priesthood was not an uncommon path for second and third sons of a lord.

"Since I possess mana, a noble son like me could have joined the Knights Templar, but that would have meant cutting ties with my house. I could have tried ascending through the upper ranks of priesthood, but that just wasn't for me. I also could have furthered my priestly studies by traveling the land as a scholar. To be honest, I was interested in such a direction, but my brothers wanted me to return home after my training."

That rat-priest was definitely hoping to climb the ranks. If he made it all the way to high priest, he would have even more influence than any of the lords. As this young man had said, he himself didn't seem a good fit for that world, and he had instead dreamed of becoming a scholar. Come to think of it, the priest who had come to teach me history had also called himself a scholar.

"What exactly does such a scholar do?"

"Most of them research war ceremonies or interpret sacred texts. Some deeply examine the rules God imposed upon this world."

So their main fields of study were scriptures and magic, both of these being the primary sources of the temple's authority. Priests who became adept at protective magic were then lent to lords whenever they endeavored to subjugate orcs or quell rebellions.

"Are there any scholars who specifically study orcs?" I asked. As interested as I was in how magic worked here, this was what I wanted to know most.

"Orcs? Those filthy things?"

"Yes."

"I'm not sure. I don't know too much about scholars, myself.

They tend to be rather detached from the secular world, but perhaps there are some who study that area."

"I see."

The standing of scholars seemed to be consistent among most worlds.

"I apologize for not being more informative," George said sullenly.

We had gotten off track. I was supposed to be considering what job to give him. Unfortunately, I didn't think that I had any priestly position to offer. In any case, I'd leave this matter to Torson.

Torson looked at me dubiously upon seeing the bruised young man I'd brought back with me. "Hero, who might this be?"

"His name is George. It's a little convoluted, but the short of it is that I've brought him here from Kerulgarz."

"I see."

I thought I saw Torson's eyes sharpen ever so slightly. Perhaps he smelled something amiss. While his clothes were in a shabby state, George had no way of masking the hints of his noble upbringing. Anyone would have questions, spoken or unspoken, to see someone like this emerge from a war zone.

"And what can we do for Sir George, then?"

"He has nowhere to return to. Please find him work."

"Work, is it?"

Torson looked at George thoughtfully. He asked me, "You're not looking for a personal attendant, are you?"

"Not really."

I didn't mind having someone attending to me, but I couldn't take him anywhere if he couldn't ride dragons. Additionally, there was no telling who might drop by at the manor, given my position; they'd likely come face-to-face with my personal attendant at some point. One such visitor might recognize the face of Gils, son of the former lord of Kerulgarz. I couldn't let my guard down with the temple either.

"Can you read and write?" Torson asked him.

"Yes." George meekly nodded.

"What about math?"

"I can do math."

"Then you'll be my own assistant for now. I'll watch how you do and decide your future work from there. How does that sound?"

I had no objections to that, nor did George.

With my mission in Kerulgarz completed, that fulfilled my current assignment from His Majesty. I decided to take it easy in my own territory for a while. If I were to head for the capital, I got the feeling I would just be summoned right back here again to deal with some new trouble. It wasn't so easy to call for me out here; they'd need a dragon rider just to send a message. Anyway, there was something I'd been meaning to test out here in Kadann Hill.

PLANET OF THE ORCS

CHAPTER 3

ORC JOHNNY

THE DAY AFTER I returned, I rode a horse out to the mill. It wasn't dragon-riding distance, and I didn't want to spook the orcs. In preparation for peace that would surely come someday, I was considering establishing communication with them.

Once there, I asked one of the workers, "Is Ruma here?"

Ruma, the manager of the flour mill, was in the process of unchaining the orcs from the mill's central pillar. Everyone was about to go on break, so my timing was perfect.

He shot me a dubious look. "Hey, Field Marshal. Need something?"

"Please lend me one of the orcs for a bit."

"Well, they do belong to you..." Strictly speaking, it was His Majesty who owned them, and who allowed me to make use of them. "But what do you need it for?"

Was I better off explaining? No, he didn't need to know my reasons. He might think me a lunatic if I told him I wanted to learn to talk like an orc.

"I thought I'd teach it some tricks to kill time," I said, without giving my words much thought.

Despite the odd look he gave me, Ruma soon brought out a small, thin orc. It was likely the weakest of his laborers, and hence its absence would have minimal impact on work. Seeing this, the other orcs suddenly began to oink. They seemed to be protesting, perhaps thinking that something terrible was in store for their comrade. Ruma cracked his whip against the floor, and the dramatic sound it made subdued their cries until they fell back into silence.

It occurred to me that I could see neither hair nor hide of the one who'd collapsed the last time I'd been here. It wasn't as if I could tell one orc from another, so I couldn't be certain, but in doing a headcount, I deduced there were two fewer orcs than there had been previously.

"What happened to the one who collapsed the last time I was here?"

"Oh, it died right after that." Ruma seemed to shrink back as he told me this, as if he feared I'd scold him.

"That's a shame. Well, there's not much we could have done." That orc had clearly been on the verge of death anyway. "From now on, though, please take care that we don't lose others."

Ruma looked relieved as he replied, "Yessir, got it, sir. So will this one suffice?" He gave the runty orc a nudge forward.

"Yes, thanks."

"Just wait a tick, and I'll leash it up for you."

Ruma fastened a collar and chain to the orc, then handed me the key.

"Don't let it slip away, now."

"I'll be careful. Also, I'd like to make use of a structure with a roof."

"There's the shed I sleep in, I guess," Ruma proposed uncomfortably.

"A storehouse would be better."

Again Ruma looked relieved, clearly not wanting an orc anywhere near where he slept. Well, I didn't want to go near his bed either.

"You can use our storehouses however you'd like. The one on the right's for wheat, and the one on the left's for the orcs' feed. Over there, that's their pen. I don't recommend that one; it stinks."

I led the orc into the storehouse for wheat. To the left were piles of unstripped wheat, while stripped wheat was heaped to the right. The air was filled with floating granules, and our feet left shallow footprints. Would it have been better to use the storehouse for feed? Then again, from what I could tell, the orcs were clearly hungry; they were probably only given the minimum necessary sustenance. I wouldn't want this one to lose concentration, being surrounded by food.

I glanced at the orc, and I could see clear fear in its eyes at having been dragged in here by someone wearing a sword. I would have to begin by easing its anxiety. First, a gentle smile... No, that wasn't the wisest idea. Smiles only worked with humans, or races very closely related to humans. With our appearances being so different, a smile might even have the opposite effect. Some races interpreted a smile as a human baring their fangs. Both of us needed to learn more about the other's expressions.

Therefore, I kept my face blank as I removed its collar. Then I offered an apple I'd brought with me for this purpose. The orc didn't take it, but I wasn't surprised. I produced a knife and cut the apple in half.

The orc recoiled a little at the sight of the blade. Once I'd tucked the knife away and bitten into my half of the fruit, I held the other half out again. Finally, the orc hesitantly reached out. With the offering in its hands, it stared at me nervously. I pointed at its apple piece and then to its mouth. The message got through this time and the orc timidly took its first bite, then hastily devoured the rest.

Not bad for first contact. I moved on to a greeting.

"Hello. Good day. Can you understand what I'm saying?"

The orc stopped eating and stared, but it was clear it didn't understand my words. This attempt at communication seemed to fall outside the scope of my translation abilities. I wasn't surprised, though, as I'd heard orcs speak before, and they were never translated. In most cases, my translation ability only applied to the language of whatever people had summoned me to their world. Beyond that, I would have to actually learn the different languages of that world, and because of this, learning languages had become one of my talents.

Unfortunately, learning orcish seemed like it would prove more difficult than any language I had tackled. First off, there were no translators who could help me along the way. The biggest obstacle, however, had to be the difficulty of differentiating and reproducing orcish vocalizations. An orc's vocal cords were not in the throat but closer to the nose, meaning they communicated through a series of snorts.

First, I pointed to myself and said my own name. Next, I pointed at the orc and urged it to introduce itself. I had to repeat this prompting several times, but it finally picked up my intent and replied with a complicated series of snorts. If I were to force the sounds into letters, it might look like: "Fguboorrrbubrooo," but it sounded different every time the orc repeated it, so I wasn't confident in my interpretation.

To make things easier, I began to think of this orc as "Johnny."

Next, I put the knife and apple side by side and pointed at them in a similar fashion. Johnny snorted at each item. I could tell the sounds were different, but I would be hard-pressed to remember or recognize them. I would hardly need to explain what happened when I attempted the vocalizations myself. Our anatomies were simply too different, and there was nothing to be done about that. Luckily, though, the orc seemed to be able to distinguish between my words to some degree. At the very least, it soon learned the difference between *knife* and *apple*.

After that, I made it my habit to go to the wheat shed with Johnny every day. It wasn't as if I currently had anything better to do.

Johnny learned fast. I had to wonder if he was a younger orc, which might have explained why he was on the small side, but I couldn't tell the young from the old and could only guess. I brought various items into the storehouse to be identified, and I taught him that his new name was Johnny. Gradually, he learned the function of several verbs. Now he could understand simple commands such as "Bring me the bucket," or "Line up three stones."

When I demonstrated my results to Ruma, his eyes grew wide as saucers. Behind him, George also seemed to take great interest in these accomplishments. Lately, he'd been helping out at the mill. He was wary of people, and thus found it easier to work among the orcs. Initially, he'd been afraid of them; he'd come a long way.

"M-milord, could I try that?" George timidly asked me.

"Go right ahead."

With my permission, he came over to me, shy but good-natured. He smiled more these days.

"Hey! Bring me the bucket!" George shouted, but Johnny remained immobile, a vacant look on his face. "Can't you hear me? Bring that bucket over here!" he cried again, to no avail. In fact, Johnny was starting to look a little fearful of George.

"How about speaking a little slower?" I suggested. "He might not understand you."

"Yes, sir." Then to Johnny: "Bring. Me. The. Bucket."

This time, he spoke calmly and soothingly, making each word distinct, and yet Johnny still didn't budge.

I commanded, "Johnny, bring me the bucket."

Johnny immediately reacted to my words. Ruma, who had

watched over the entire exchange, gaped in astonishment as the orc raced to me with bucket in hand.

"Wow, being a hero helps. What magic did you use?"

"No, I didn't use any—"

Then I understood. Thanks to the translation process, Ruma and George heard me as though I were speaking their own language. However, as this didn't apply to the orcs, to Johnny, I must have come off as speaking in Japanese. That meant I had inadvertently taught Johnny Japanese, which was a useless skill in this world. It seemed like it would be too much work to get Ruma to understand my explanation, so I decided to make the most of the confusion.

"I guess God's chosen hero can even get orcs to follow him."

Ruma looked quite impressed, while George seemed a little sulky.

All of this was only the first step toward my goal. To ultimately negotiate with the orcs, I would need to train an orc translator who understood what I was saying completely. We were currently at a handful of nouns and simple verbs, so at this point, peace negotiations with the orcs were still a dream.

For now, my methods were limited to gestures and whatever objects I had on hand. I wanted to convey more abstract words like "country" and "peace," which I would need to do in order to pursue my goal, but hadn't the slightest idea how to link those complex concepts to simple words. I was frustrated with my own lack of imagination.

There was another critical problem. I had proven I could teach orcs my own words, but I still couldn't understand theirs.

I would have Johnny repeat the same words to me over and over, but it always came across to me as nearly indistinguishable grunting. It was possible we didn't even share the same range of hearing, which would make my efforts at understanding him all the more futile. Even if Johnny understood what I said, this endeavor was pointless if our communication didn't go both ways.

I considered, then, that perhaps we could make do with written words instead. Still, whether I taught him my written language or learned his, it would take a considerable amount of time.

My mind was occupied with these challenges when I heard the beating of approaching hooves. I lifted my head to a terrible intuition, and there was Meg, just as I had expected. As usual, she had brought along her entourage of cross-dressed maids. Honestly, she had good taste. What was this about, though?

"Good day to you, Hero."

Having dismounted from her horse, Meg saluted me. George had hidden behind me the moment he realized who she was, but it was already too late. When Meg saw him, I saw a sparkle come to her eyes. Had they met before?

I asked, "Do you need something?"

"I'm just checking in with you. I heard you'd hired a new vassal." She took a peek behind me. George turned the other way in a futile effort to avoid her probing eyes. She said to him, "A pleasure to make your acquaintance. What's your name?" Her wide smile told me she already knew the answer.

"It's Gi—George," he answered curtly, his face still turned to one side.

For his part, Ruma looked touched, as if he were witnessing young love in bloom, though I sensed this situation was nowhere near what the good man had in mind. He said, "C'mon, George, a lovely lady is talking to you. How about you look her in the eye?" Ruma thought he was doing George a favor and didn't realize he was just backing the young man even further into a corner.

"That's all right." Meg then turned to me. "Hey, Hero, what are you going to use him for?"

"I don't have a firm plan yet. For now, I've left him in Torson's care until he finds a job that suits him."

"Hmm... Would you give him to me, then? I've already taken a liking to him."

She'd said this with a shining smile, but George only looked at me pleadingly.

"Not going to happen," I told her. She wasn't taking George away from me. I couldn't begin to fathom what she had in mind for him. I wasn't even swayed by her cutesy sulking expression.

Ruma came closer to me, and timidly said, "U-um, milord..."

"What is it?"

"I know it's not my place to speak, but it's about George. If Megriel has taken to him, then he could have a far brighter future working for her, rather than grinding wheat or doing similar menial labor. Not to mention..." He glanced at Meg, then whispered, "...she's such a lovely lady, I'm sure George would be quite happy."

I could tell Ruma truly had good intentions.

Meg chimed in, "He's completely right, Hero! I wouldn't treat George poorly. I'm sure I could greatly benefit him in the long run. In fact, I'll personally see to it that he receives the promotion of his life!"

"And just what sort of promotion is that? The lord of a certain territory, perhaps?"

"Yeah, maybe something like that. It's what all men strive for," Meg said.

That cemented it for me. "Not in a million years," I declared, shielding George with my back. Like hell I would allow George to become such a high-profile figure that old feuds would resurface. I had other things to deal with.

"A pity."

Her features drooped, and her shoulders slumped as well. Ruma seemed to want to say something, but he held his tongue. Meanwhile, I heard George sigh in relief from behind me.

Meg said, "Incidentally, that one's from the mill, right? Are you sure you should let it move around freely like that?"

She gestured at the small orc who had drawn nearer to me, holding a bucket. What perfect timing. I decided to show off the fruits of my labor.

"That's no ordinary orc. It's an orc who can follow spoken commands!"

I ordered Johnny to place three apples in a row. He hurried to the wheat storeroom, then returned with three apples and promptly set them down in a line.

Meg said, "Oh, that's quite something."

"Isn't it?"

Johnny was no doubt hungry, but had controlled himself.

Anyway, whenever the lessons went well, I'd let him keep the apples afterward. He never ate them himself, but instead brought them to share with the other orcs, which I found admirable.

"So what are you going to do with him?"

Well, I had a grand goal, but I knew peace with the orcs wouldn't please Meg. In fact, if she learned of my plan, she might actively get in my way. I considered my response, and it seemed she misunderstood my silence.

"You sure have it nice, Hero. You obviously have plenty of free time on your hands. Myself, I've been running around day and night pursuing my duties, with barely any time to sleep."

"You did that to yourself. Trust me, I have my reasons. I'm not just playing around."

"Well let's hear them, then."

I threw together an explanation that might satisfy her. "I'm researching to see if we can weaponize orcs to make up for our shortage of human troops."

Just the sort she might approve of. What could she complain about now?

"Umm...if it's troops you need, do you want to borrow some of my people?"

It was almost like there was pity in her eyes. Rather than approve of my fake goal, she looked doubtful that I could train orcs to fight for us. To be honest, I shared that opinion.

I told her, "No, I'm fine."

"Really? Very well. Oh, by the way, I hear the temple is on edge thanks to that little festival of yours."

I pressed her for more details. As it turned out, the ruckus caused when Veralgon burned the mountain of orc goods had been interpreted as: *the Hero's ceremony to dispel an orcish curse.* I remembered the rat-priest accusing me of blasphemy.

Meg said, "The temple gets agitated whenever paganism crops up. It will make matters worse if they catch wind of you getting along with orcs." She glanced at Johnny. "You should really keep these things behind closed doors."

Just then, a massive shadow passed overhead. I looked up to see a dragon descending toward the manor.

"Oh, that must be a messenger from the capital," Meg said gleefully, her eyes following the dragon's flight path. "Let's hurry back, Hero! Can I hear the message with you?"

Her timing was a little too good, and I figured she must have known that a messenger was coming.

On the northern edge of the hero's territory, the margrave's city was filled with joy and festivities, their army having made a triumphant return. The orcish soldiers who had smashed through the pesky human forces now proudly paraded down the main street.

Boldly presented at the head of this procession were the severed heads of three fearsome monsters, hoisted high by fifty gunners. These heads were all that remained of the vile dragons that had terrorized the northern settlements, and a symbol of the brave militia who had brought about their end. The militia's uniforms, marred by bullet holes, mud, and shoddy patchwork, gave them the appearance of seasoned veterans, despite their being a long way from the standing army. In exchange for their service, they would receive tax exemption and a claim to the wastelands of the north. Their martial achievements aside, they were always fighting to protect their own homes, so their motivation was generally more passionate than that of the average soldier.

The militia was followed by the many soldiers who had taken part in the great battle—a battle that had yet to be given a formal name.

The standing army appeared about halfway down the procession. Unlike the soldiers who tramped along ahead of them, the standing army marched in perfect unison. They were made up of the elites of the margrave's army, and in the great battle, they were the ones who had demolished the human cavalry and thus cemented victory. When these elites showed up with their spoils—a parade float piled high with helmets stripped off of human heads—the onlookers erupted into cheers.

But the real climax came after that. The float was immediately followed by a white steed ridden by the army's supreme commander, and then a study cage on wheels with a single human inside. Judging by their ornamented gear, this prisoner was presumably of high status. Watched over by the very best of the standing army, this captive was the true centerpiece of the parade. A mix of cheers for the commander and angry roars toward the prisoner filled the air.

This noise reached all the way beyond the city's walls to the distant army barracks.

It was there that the Black Dog listened to the commotion with gritted teeth. Why, the supreme commander hadn't been anywhere near the battlefield. It was absurd to even call this a victory.

Yes, the orcs had managed to defeat their enemies in that battle, but they had failed their objective of breaching the valley, and many villages had fallen victim to dragon attacks. Consequently, farmers turned refugees had flooded into the city and were likely unwilling to return to their farms. There had been casualties in regions previously considered relatively safe from air raids. Fearing more such raids, a good number of people had abandoned perfectly intact villages to flee here. The city couldn't depend on previous harvests to feed these many refugees, and with many farmlands decimated or abandoned, the yield of the margrave's territory would inevitably fall into sharp decline.

Large-scale rationing had been implemented to address the worsening food shortage. The city had even been forced to access the army's food reserves, and because of this, major military deployment would likely be impossible for a while to come.

Still, even if it had been a victory of sorts, why was a key figure like the Black Dog here at the barracks and not a participant in the celebration? The answer was simple. He and his riders, as well as all the other mercenary tribes, had been prohibited from appearing in the parade. There was no doubt in his mind that this was handiwork of the margrave's lazy son.

"Barbarians shall not be allowed within the margrave's walls," was the official reason, despite the imperial law that proclaimed all people were equal before the emperor. Surely if the margrave had heard of this exclusion, he would have given him a good kick in the rear, no matter how much he doted on his son.

Unfortunately, the margrave had been bedridden from illness for a while now. The Black Dog had heard rumors that his time of death was near. These rumors had crushed his spirit. Like the others of his tribe, the Black Dog had been raised on the heroic tales of distant ancestors. There'd been a time when his ancestors, riding their fearsome aquilup mounts, had laid waste to the countries of the plains. Some had even claimed land of their own and become rulers. The Black Dog still looked up to the heroes of those days.

Of course, those days were no more than a dream now. It had been several hundred years since his tribe had bent their knees to the empire. He had long since abandoned his grandiose dream of forming a kingdom of his own, but his ambition had yet to fade fully. His desire to make a name for himself still burned within him, and it was not impossible for him to achieve renown on the battlefield. Plenty of his tribe had managed it, including his great-uncle.

During the last civil war, his great-uncle had been hired by the previous emperor—only a prince at the time—and had ended up as His Majesty's right-hand man. His great-uncle went on to become a count and lead the Imperial Aquilup Regiment. Despite hailing from a border tribe, he had paved a path to his own success. The Black Dog aspired to be like him one day. And yet, by the time he'd left his homeland, chasing the dreams of his great-uncle, the wars were already ending. He'd gone from land to land, hunting down bandits and the remnants of the revolts. The group he'd formed with his ten closest friends had grown into an aquilup cavalry fifty riders strong, and yet the grand battles he hoped for still weren't there. The wars were over, and the ashes had gone cold. The bandits were few and far between. As far as the empire was concerned, mercenaries like him were no longer needed.

The Black Dog had finally found his place here, in the northern territory. On the undeveloped plain where the hairless monkeys ran rampant, he had finally gained a proper mission.

By piling up numerous successes against the humans, he had earned the trust of the margrave and his staff. On the last large-scale expedition, he had essentially been entrusted with the command of the entire army. In those northern lands, he had almost fulfilled his dreams, but his status had ultimately proved a candle in the wind. One might say it had been an anomaly for him to have been welcomed so warmly in the first place.

The margrave's son wasn't as kind to him as the father had been. The son plainly hated the Black Dog, being too small-minded to even acknowledge the achievements of one who had been such an asset. His noble lineage made him even more of a pest.

But this didn't mean the Black Dog could simply leave these lands. The east and west had largely stabilized, and public order was improving all throughout the lands. Despite having distinguished himself in skirmishes with the humans, that hadn't been enough to net him a high position. His great accomplishment, of tipping the scales in the battle, had somehow become the margrave's son's accomplishment.

There was also the fact that he had renewed his mercenary contract only the year before, since he hadn't expected the margrave's condition to take such a turn. Ending such a contract prematurely would be a lethal blow to his credibility. Therefore, he was obligated to work for at least another five years under that idiot son. Still, he sometimes contemplated just throwing everything away and returning home. After all, he had enough funds to buy a small farm, and he could find himself a wife and spend his days tilling the fields. One day, he could sit down by the fireplace and tell his kids and grandkids about his past adventures.

But this idyllic dream was impossible, and the Black Dog knew it. He had learned the enticing taste of what lay between life and death. At this point, he would no longer be able to endure such a bucolic life. The doors to such a destiny were all closed. Was there nothing he could do but remain here and be worked to death by the idiot son? As the Black Dog reflected fatalistically about his future, a messenger came from the margrave. This was one of the margrave's closest aides, and the Black Dog knew him well.

The aide said, "Our lord has regained consciousness, and he's calling for you."

Having relayed the message, the aide immediately turned and urged the Black Dog to follow.

PLANET OF THE ORCS

CHAPTER 4

SCHOLARS AND CEREMONIES

PRIESTS HAD FORMED a long queue in front of a small tower. It was a rather inconspicuous lookout tower west of Dragonjaw Gate, only around seven meters high and maybe six meters in diameter. And yet, priest after priest after priest continued to be swallowed up within.

"That's incredible. Where do these people disappear to?" Meg asked, eyes wide. So far, she had seen more than a thousand priests climb those stairs, and not one of them had reappeared.

I explained, "The magic circle is underground, but the entrance to the chamber is inside that tower."

Inside the tower was a bizarre statue. Lifting it away would reveal a secret stairway to a subterranean chamber containing a massive magic circle—the room in which I'd first opened my eyes to when I'd been summoned to the world.

"I see...so they purposely chose this high spot to hide a passage underground," she said, impressed.

The dragon rider who'd arrived the other day had been, as expected, a messenger from His Majesty. Preparations to restore Dragonjaw Gate's barrier, which had fallen due to orc bombardment, had been completed. As I was in charge of the nation's military, it was my job to oversee the ceremony.

It was that responsibility that had brought me here, but why was Meg here as well? After hearing the rider's message with me, she had obstinately insisted that she witness the ceremony too. It just sounded like an annoyance to me, so of course I refused. Initially.

"I'm the only one he called for," I told her. "I'll go alone."

But Meg was not so easily dissuaded, and she insisted that she would come along as my attendant. She argued, "The nation's esteemed field marshal should not be seen going about without a single attendant!"

"You think so? I see Rigel out and about on his own all the time."

Rigel occasionally took dragon keepers with him when he flew, but dragon keepers were dragon keepers, not attendants. They always remained with the dragons.

Meg countered, "Dragon riders are different. Many of them are commoners by birth, and they use dragons to get around, so they're rarely in danger. But you, with your status, should be accompanied by an attendant or two."

"I get around by dragon too. I should be fine."

"It's no good! You're the field marshal! The representative of His Majesty! This isn't like your last trip, where you were just listening to a treaty!"

"But it would be a pain to have to travel by horse just to accommodate an attendant."

"That's where I come in! I ride dragons, and I served the princess, so I have perfected the proper etiquette of a knight's attendant. There are dragon keepers permanently stationed at Dragonjaw Gate, so you don't have to bring one yourself. You have space for one rider, and that could be me. What do you say?" She proudly stuck out her chest, and seeing its splendor did sway me ever so slightly.

"You're currently Lord Proxy. You're not in a position to act as a mere attendant."

"Not true at all. When they travel, important figures usually bring along subordinates with high positions. Why, my father always bragged how he was expected to serve the previous king his wine."

She sulked, cried, laughed, smiled, flailed her arms, and did everything in her power to make my life difficult. Eventually, wearied but not seduced, I gave in to her persistence and agreed to let her ride behind me. With the utmost reluctance, I must add.

"It must be nice, being so free," I found myself muttering as I stared at the disappearing line of priests.

"Are you talking about me?" Meg looked taken aback.

"Yeah, that's right."

"I'm not sure I'm all that free, being a woman. For instance, women can have quite a hard time choosing their destiny in marriage, you know. Rather, you seem far freer to me."

"I only seem free because I have nothing in this world. Given time, I'll have so many obligations placed on me, I won't be able to move a muscle anymore."

"Then you're the same as me. Enduring nothing but bothersome customs, conventions, and laws. Being a woman makes it hard for me to even gather up a small army."

She thrust out her lips in a pout.

I replied, "While you find common sense and basic expectations to be bothersome, you've never let them tie you down. You do your best to slip around them, or else ignore them entirely."

"You make me sound like a failure of a human being," Meg said, taking offense.

She was a failure, in a sense. But I continued, "That's what they call freedom. Those people who fail to give in to conventional limitations, who won't accept the standards that are imposed on them."

Humans couldn't fly. This seemed an immutable limitation, so long as gravity held them down. Only those who refused to give in to that limitation—be it through magic or machinery—made it into the sky.

"That is one way of looking at it, I suppose. It's not like I've actually been chained down or anything. But if we're talking about freedom, you yourself could choose to live free, Hero. You don't even have to wait for it; you could begin right now."

"You're right. And yet not."

What she said was true on a surface level, but people with leadership responsibilities like me and Thret just couldn't afford to be free in that sense. In fact, the world would be in chaos if each and every person lived free of conventional obligations.

"Y'know, Hero, I was convinced you were the same sort of person as me."

"What do you mean by that?"

"What *could* I mean by that?"

She tilted her head cutely. I sighed.

The line of priests went on and on. The stairway leading down through the tower was rather narrow, after all.

"Come to think of it, you came from a different world, didn't you?"

"Yeah, I did."

"What sort of world was it?"

"Civilization was far more developed there than it is here, and I can't even compare the level of comfort. You could drink safe, clean water anywhere with just a twist of a knob. A house could become warmer or cooler with just the flick of a finger."

"You must have come from quite a nice place," she said enviously.

"Yeah, and it was peaceful too." At least, the country I'd been born into.

"Then it seems my own world is better suited for me." The

notion of peace was enough to make her lose interest. "Do you want to go back?"

I was just about to reply, "Of course." Instead, I hesitated for a moment. "Yeah, I do."

"You paused there. I knew it—peace just isn't enough," Meg stated happily.

"Quit making me sound like a war addict."

"You're not?"

"I'm not."

"Then I see no other reason for you to want to remain here. You could be living as a hero in a far more comfortable world than this one, right?"

"I'm not a hero in my own world."

"Really? Even after saving so many other worlds?"

It seemed Meg had completely misunderstood my situation.

"In my original world, no one believes you when you tell them you've saved other realms, especially when you don't have any evidence or witnesses to back up your claims. It isn't any different here, though. Say someone mysteriously disappeared, then suddenly returned one day to announce, 'I'm back from another world!' They'd be seen as a lunatic."

"Then how did you live there?"

"Dangling off my parents' legs, without a proper job to my name."

"Seriously?"

"Well, I wasn't unemployed by choice. I kept getting called to other worlds, so I could never hold a proper job."

Who in their right mind would hire someone without a degree or prior work history, who was prone to disappearing without a trace? Honestly, though my original world was comfortable, it was not welcoming.

In these other worlds, I could ride dragons. I could pilot golems equipped with ancient armaments. I could wield legendary weapons. Back home, they wouldn't even let me manage a parking lot. A kid who shined shoes for a living would have it better than me. No, if possible I wanted to stay in *these* worlds. Of course, it didn't quite work that way. Once one of these worlds was saved, I would be forced back to my own...and if I tried to remain by refusing to save it, then that world faced total annihilation.

There weren't any worlds I had a particular attachment to, but it was only human to want to save them anyway. Luckily, I hadn't failed yet. In the first place, there was no reason for me to remain in a world once—

"You're quite skilled at martial arts, aren't you?"

Meg's question kept my thoughts from straying too far.

"Last I was there, my world was at peace. Being trained to kill people wouldn't help me find a job. I don't say professional fighters were unnecessary, even at peacetime, but the governments and companies that retained them wouldn't want someone who keeps disappearing."

Respectable organizations that employed such individuals for security were closely regulated, but then there were criminal organizations that might prove an alternative. For me, though, that avenue was out of the question.

"Looks like you have it hard, then, in the grander scheme of things," she said sympathetically. It seemed the message had gotten through.

"That's something I have no power over," I said, looking into the sky.

It had taken a while, but the line was finally quite a bit shorter. I'd been distracted by opening up about myself—to Meg, of all people. It irked me how everything I'd said might lower her estimation of me.

In any case, she was correct in pointing out that I had difficulty living in a peaceful world. Not just because I'd been jobless and without a place of my own. If I had to admit it, I was simply bored there. No matter what I did, I didn't feel stimulated. Well, that wasn't entirely true. For example, I enjoyed delicious food and interesting anime. Such mundanities would stave off the boredom to some small degree.

It hadn't always been like this. At least, it wasn't before I returned from my first adventure. Prior to that, I could remember experiencing joy, fun, and sadness...all the various ups and downs of everyday life. Gradually, though, things had changed.

I'd finally become aware of it after returning from the fourth or fifth world. I wondered if my brain had been fried from exposing myself to so many perilous situations. I realized I now thrived on danger, and the more danger the better. It wasn't that I wanted to die. I wanted to live, but I could only ever feel alive when I was dancing with death.

Nowadays, I felt more truly alive in these other worlds. Every place I was sent to was filled with danger and adventure. I could sense the seams coming undone even in those worlds that at first glance appeared safe and secure, and this made for a nice sense of tension. Troublingly enough, whoever was sending me to these worlds had become both the root of all evil and my sole salvation.

I didn't intend to open up to Meg any more than I already had, lest she start acting all smug on me. I wasn't like her. I didn't actively cause battles for my own sake. I intended to fight as a hero until the end. While the only worth to my existence might be found in battle, I still wanted to remain human. I would fight only to save a world and its people. Drawing the line there kept me sane.

No... we were worlds apart, Meg and I, and she would never truly know about me. Still, if I strayed from the path I'd set for myself, I had a feeling it would sadden her.

"Hey, Hero. Looks like it's our turn."

When I looked up, I saw the last priest disappear into the tower.

"You're right."

We followed behind him, into the tower, then down into the underground chamber.

Though the chamber beneath Dragonjaw Gate was vast, the several thousand priests who filled the space made it feel cramped. Back when I'd been summoned here, the whole place had been filled with a pale blue light emitted by a complicated magic circle.

However, that circle had lost its light, so the chamber was illuminated by the lanterns that the priests carried.

"What are they going to do, I wonder?" Meg muttered impatiently as she watched the gathered priests. What was with her attitude? She was the one who'd said she wanted to see the ceremony. Granted, the proceedings had been rather boring so far.

This wasn't what I'd expected when I'd heard a ceremony was to be held. There was no singing to God, nor any dancing, and of course there were no sacrifices. Some priests kneeled here and there, drawing small magic circles within the greater circle, murmuring chants or spells as they placed their hands on the fresh symbols. At times, a priest would abandon his own circle and go off somewhere, and then a different priest who'd previously been standing by would assume his place and begin murmuring something else. Seeing that the priests who stood were swaying on their feet, I guessed they were sending mana into the great circle.

"Would you like an explanation?" came a voice from behind me.

I turned to discover an elderly priest with a serious face. I assumed from the two younger priests attending him that he had a bit of status.

"Yes, if you would. Bur first, could I get your name?"

"My apologies. I lead the temple scholars. My name is Worion. I am responsible for overseeing this ceremony."

I'd heard that the scholars were priests who conducted various forms of research for the temple. To compare to my own world, they were something along the lines of national researchers.

"I've no doubt this ceremony is the result of years of research by your scholars, so it's an honor to hear the details from someone as prestigious as yourself. What are the priests doing right now?"

The head scholar replied solemnly, "They're pouring mana into the circle."

Just as I'd guessed.

"Wait, that's it?" Meg blurted. Perhaps an attendant who intruded on their lord's conversations lacked a bit of self-awareness.

"Yes, that's *it*, young lady," Worion calmly replied. He likely didn't know who she was, or else he wouldn't have called the Proxy Lord of Morsharz *young lady*. "It may not seem like much to you, but it took us more time than you can imagine to conclude that this was how we should proceed."

I was beginning to wonder what others thought of me, leading around a cross-dressed young woman of marriageable age as my attendant.

The priest explained, "At first, we had absolutely no knowledge about the magic circle's functions. Even now, we don't understand what a majority of its symbols mean. It was only recently that we determined the right points at which to inject mana."

He pointed at his feet. "Take this symbol, for instance. It is repeated in two hundred and forty-three places on the circle, but it is still uncertain exactly what it does. The fact that we can carry out the ceremony despite our imperfect understanding is thanks to the work of the former head scholar, Saint Magos. He managed to partially decipher a number of documents retrieved from the old capital, though, of course, much in those documents remains to be decrypted. By carefully comparing the diagrams with his own knowledge of magic circles, he formed a theory on how to incorporate the mana from ley lines into fundamental charging points. Thereby—"

Worion's tone was gaining in intensity. Once he got going on this subject that he felt so passionate about, I could tell he wouldn't stop.

When I saw him pause to take a breath, I interrupted him. "I see. Could I ask more about what's being done now, specifically?"

"Hero, are you aware of the Saint Boregan's Chalice?"

"No, sorry, I haven't been in this world very long."

"Of course. How about you, young lady?"

I saw his stern old face grow somewhat softer, as if he were looking at a granddaughter. *Don't be fooled by her appearance*, I warned him in my head. Perhaps Meg looked like a good-natured young lady, but she was exactly the sort one needed to remain wary of.

"Yes," she said. "It's used at the start of every year."

Worion seemed satisfied by her simple answer, and he carried on with his explanation.

"It is said that the chalice was designed by Saint Boregan, who was head scholar ten generations ago. It was meant to caution and teach the greedy. As for what it actually is, it would probably be easier if I showed you."

Worion turned and gave an order, and shortly, two of his attendants came forward carrying a peculiar cup and a pitcher.

"This is Saint Boregan's Chalice. Hold it, if you'd like."

The metal chalice was deep and strangely shaped, featuring a column in the center of its bowl with an elaborate dragon head at the top. I flipped the cup over and found a hole in the base. Some sort of tube seemed to run through it. From what I could tell, the object didn't give off any mana. In what way was this artifact supposed to instruct the greedy?

"Please, play the part of a greedy man, and pour as much drink as you'd like."

This time I was handed the pitcher. There wasn't anything strange about it, no odd details or features. It contained only water, but for the sake of his demonstration, I was no doubt meant to pretend it was wine.

I carefully filled the cup to about half. Nothing unusual occurred.

"Remember, you are a greedy drinker. Would such a small amount satisfy you?"

At Worion's urging, I poured more, and all of a sudden the chalice began to empty at the bottom. I stopped pouring to see if that would change anything, but the water continued to flow, and in no time, the cup was empty.

"Isn't that interesting? If your greed gets the better of you, you lose all you had."

I examined the cup further, and this time, I noticed a small hole at the base of the column inside the cup as well. So, it was a siphon. Now that I thought of it, I was aware of similar novelty items in my own world. They were called Pythagorean cups, or greedy cups.

I said, "There's a space inside the column with a pipe that runs from the base to the top, where it turns and runs toward the bottom of the cup."

"What sharp eyes you have, Hero. You're precisely right. If the cup is filled beyond a certain point, the liquid will be forced up and then down through the column and emerge underneath."

I remembered hearing something back in school about the trick having to do with fluid mechanics and gravity. Did they understand the actual physics here?

"A similar phenomenon can be created using a chain. First, you coil a chain on a high platform, then lift one of its ends even higher. Then, release that end over the edge of the platform. The rest of the chain will climb up to the end's original height, then flow downward in a self-pouring fountain until all the chain runs out. Something like this occurs with mana, but in this case, height is not physical height but a certain concentration of mana."

This explanation didn't seem to register with Meg, who had tilted her head as she listened in on the conversation. To be honest, I didn't completely get it either, but I understood the gist of what he was illustrating.

"In short, you're pouring in mana to fill the pipe to the point of redirection."

"As expected of a hero. You catch on quickly."

If the amount of mana directed by the priests exceeded a certain threshold, apparently the mana of the land's ley lines would begin flooding over into the magic circle. For once, knowledge from my old world was proving useful.

"How much mana will you need to restart it?"

"Yes, well, we were able to gather more priests than anticipated, so..." The head scholar thought for a moment. "Three months of work should do it. We will likely finish before the snow thaws."

A kneeling priest with a face pale from effort stood up and staggered over to a rest area. Another priest quickly occupied his vacancy to keep the pouring of mana unbroken.

Three months of this? It was going to be a harsh winter for these clergymen.

Dragonjaw Gate was the massive fortress that protected the humans' territory. The priests' ceremony would reactivate the magic circle that protected the fort from all manner of projectiles. I could hardly even call it a ceremony; it was more like factory work as an army of priests simply poured in their mana on rotation. Not only was it estimated this would take at least three months of constant work, but on top of that, I learned I was supposed to remain at the fortress the entire time. As His Majesty's field marshal and the man in charge of the country's military, it was apparently my duty to oversee the process.

Despite my being a supervisor, there wasn't any work for me to do. The procedures, decisions, shifts, and stations were all managed by the temple. All that was left for me to do was occasionally stop by the main chamber and observe the priests at work. It was a monotonous business, devoting themselves to injecting their mana and only swapping out when their bodies could no longer hold up. That was all there was to it, simple but arduous.

To be honest, it wasn't the most exciting thing to watch for any length of time. In fact, I would have been more engaged watching an anthill. This thought inspired me to look around for an anthill on the ground, but perhaps due to the season, or perhaps because ants didn't exist in this world, I couldn't find any around Dragonjaw Gate.

Meg grew even more bored than me on the very first day, and she promptly decided she would return to her territory. What had happened to all that talk about serving as my attendant? She was the one who'd forced me to bring her along to witness the ceremony. What a free spirit she was. Well, neither of us had realized the procedure would go on for three months. Despite her capricious nature, she still had a relatively busy position, and she couldn't be away from her territory for too long.

She expected me to bring her to her territory myself, as if it went without saying. It was a round trip of an entire day by dragon, and while I did have some thoughts on her attitude, I had to admit it was a welcome change of pace. From that day onward during my stay, I would spend my free time walking Veralgon through the clouds. It was fun and liberating racing through the sky, but by the third day, the dragon keepers begged me to refrain.

The keepers stressed that dragons generally entered a state of hibernation during the winter. Although domesticated dragons chose to remain awake as their riders did, Veralgon was a bit different from other dragons. He was already violent, so if I kept rousing him from his torpor to engage in the physical exertion of flight, he was bound to grow increasingly displeased.

"He takes it out on us dragon keepers the moment you're out of sight, Hero. Last night, one of our young ones was actually injured. Please, don't take the dragon flying without a serious purpose."

Since an injury had occurred, I had to honor that request. So, left with little else to do, I decided to explore the fortress.

The fortress's design was basic as could be. One massive wall faced the valley and collected water from snowmelt. A gentle slope climbed from its southern border to its eastern edge. There were nine towers of varying size, from which it was possible to rain arrows and stones down upon any enemy army that might attempt to climb the slope. The largest tower was the fort's main headquarters, located at a central spot in the wall, and this was where the barracks were situated, as well. A massive water dragon was carved on the moat's sluice gate, right beneath this central tower.

The second largest tower, commonly called the Gate Tower, was at the very end of the aforementioned slope. It was through this tower that the world of humanity connected with the world beyond. It was the more heavily protected of the fort's two gateways, and had hostilities been underway, each of the tower's merlons would have sheltered an archer with bow at the ready. Adjacent to the Gate Tower was an open space where troops would assemble before embarking outside on an expedition.

While incredibly sturdy against outside forces, the Gate Tower had no defenses against attacks from within. There wasn't even a simple fence to protect it from the possibility of attack from humans. A house for dragon keepers had been erected a short distance from the tower, but this was as unguarded as the rest of it. Of course, I highly doubted anyone would attempt to steal a dragon. On a side note, atop the towers, there were only merlons and crenels for archers facing outward, not inward.

I found something else rather unexpected while investigating. As it turned out, the fortress employed orcs here and there. I spotted the first orcs as I was exploring the interior of the Gate Tower. In one chamber, orcs were chained to a thick, rotating pillar fitted with push bars situated in the middle of the floor. Here, they would be whipped into turning the device.

"This is the power source of the Gate Tower," a young soldier told me. Herbert, the captain of the garrison, had lent him to me as a guide when I'd asked for permission to look around.

"What do they power?"

The young man courteously explained, "When they turn the pillar, it winds a chain, which can raise and lower the gate. There is an identical room on the opposite side of the fortress, for that gate."

"But isn't it dangerous to use orc labor here, of all places?"

There would be quite a bit of trouble if they were to open the gate in the middle of a siege.

Before my guide could answer, an older soldier who watched over the orcs answered me with a laugh. "Sure, they're ferocious on the battlefield, but these here have all been broken in. They're harmless."

He produced an apple from a crate in the corner of the room and tossed it at the orcs. The apple landed and rolled between two of them, who immediately began scuffling for it.

"Place your bets, young'un," he said to the guide.

"Then I'll bet on the right-hand one." The guide pointed at the younger of the two orcs, but the match was soon over, and the young soldier grumbled as he handed over a coin.

"Did you see that, Hero?" the older soldier said. "They're no better than beasts. Not to mention, it's impossible to see or hear anything outside this room, so they don't know what's going on. We had no problems at all the last time orcs invaded. We're fine." He confidently tucked the coin into his pocket.

The guide added, "The gate's chain is only hooked up when necessary, and that isn't done in here. Nothing would happen even if they did start turning the post on their own. During times of emergency, we can also sever the chain to drop the gate immediately. Shall we see the next machine room, then?"

They seemed to have a well-thought-out system. Orcs were similarly used to open the water gates, and to draw well water. They were treated better than those in my own territory in that each had its own room to retire to. That said, those rooms were essentially jail cells, damp places that never saw the light of the sun. Still, it was preferable to twenty of them sleeping in a huddle, as in our orc shed. Perhaps I could use the setup here as an example in improving our orcs' conditions.

If it was not forbidden to bring orcs here, then perhaps I could fetch Johnny from Kadann Hill. Despite its size, there wasn't much for me to do in the fortress. My language lessons could help pass the time.

Thinking of the lessons reminded me of something. I had intended to ask if there were any scholar priests who studied the orcish language. I planned on seeking out Worion in the ceremony chamber, for who better to tell me?

"Could you tell me the specifics?"

Worion leaned toward me, his eyes gleaming with fiery curiosity. His sheer intensity compelled me to step back. We were in the underground chamber with its many priests conducting the ceremony around us. Unfortunately, directly behind me was a circle of these priests, praying as they channeled their mana. As I carelessly retreated from Worion, I accidentally tripped and tumbled right into their midst.

Worion rushed forward to pull me to my feet. "My apologies! I have a habit of getting overly impassioned." To the startled priests he said, "Very sorry that I disrupted your concentration. Please, take a break."

The priests who'd been caught up in my fall bowed to us and then left, quickly replaced by the next batch.

"Er, I'm not sure what to say. That was...unbecoming of me." The head scholar laughed awkwardly. We moved our conversation to a side room with a little more space. I had lit a fire under Worion by bringing up the theory of heliocentrism, simply in the course of small talk, when what I really wanted to get into was learning the orcish tongue. It was a hard subject to broach to a high-ranking priest of a faith that saw all orcs as enemies. Their texts preached: *Orcs are idiots, beasts that can't speak as men*. If I suddenly said, "I'm trying to communicate with an orc," I had no idea how he would react.

I was a little impatient at how enthusiastic he was about this other topic, but I still explained the Copernican system as best I could.

Worion said, "I see! So where you come from, the stars do not circle your world. Rather, your world makes its rounds around the sun."

"That's what I learned in school."

"I must ask about your schools! But first, about this theory..."

With his burning curiosity, this man could have become a top researcher in my world.

I cut in, "Does this world believe that the stars orbit this planet, then?"

"Yes, that's right. It's written in scripture."

Scripture, eh? It would probably be difficult to convince him of concepts that went against scripture.

He went on, "I've never thought to doubt it. Who would think that *we* were the ones traveling through the heavens? Hmm...but if you consider the movement of the planets, then certainly..."

Worion suddenly fell silent, deep in thought. I had been left on the wayside, forced to simply watch the ceremony as the many priests swapped positions to inject mana or head for the break room. I was getting bored by it already, and Worion didn't seem like he was coming back from his reverie.

"Oi! Paper! Bring me paper!" he suddenly cried out, having evidently made it back from his inner space. A boy off to one side, likely an apprentice, produced a parchment and pen form and reverently offered them. Upon receiving them, Worion set to writing feverishly, frequently dipping the pen into the inkwell the boy held for him.

"Now deliver this to our astronomy division. Tell them it's urgent."

"Right away!"

The boy took the freshly inked paper and was off like a rocket.

"Are the scriptures not absolute?" I asked Worion.

"Well, the scriptures are a collection of God's teachings, but while God's teachings are absolute, the scriptures themselves were written by human hands. There are, perhaps, some mistaken accounts, and it is our duty as scholars to correct them."

His stance on scripture was more flexible than I'd anticipated. Perhaps it would be all right, then, to discuss orcish language.

Almost casually, I asked, "Incidentally, are there any scholars who specifically study orcs?"

"Why orcs?"

"To win a war, you must first know the enemy. Is the study of orcs prohibited?"

"No, it isn't...but they are simply unclean life-forms. No one would research them by choice. In the past, an excellent study was done on their anatomy, and a few of our priests are researching the tools they make. His Majesty has given us a direct order to investigate their weapons, you see, but that black powder of theirs is an enigma, and there are a number of parts to their weapons that our blacksmiths cannot reproduce."

"What about their words? Is anyone researching their language and writing system?"

The head priest's usual serene expression suddenly disappeared. "They have no language," he said levelly. "Hence, no one studies it."

This change in attitude was unsettling, but I decided to persist just a little bit more.

"That can't be true. Look how they coordinate their forces. That would be impossible without a common tongue."

"Don't be so sure. Many beasts and birds act in packs and flocks, and they have no spoken language. The same goes for orcs." Even as he said this I got the sense he wasn't entirely convinced by his own words. "Hero, the scriptures clearly state that orcs have no intellect and thus no language."

"You just said there could be mistakes in the scriptures. Isn't it a scholar's duty to prove mistakes weren't made?"

Worion began to look bitter, as if his very faith were being challenged. He declared, "On that matter, there is no room for debate. The scriptures are correct."

Still, I suspected he held more complex thoughts on this matter than his declaration would have me believe. The religious *correct*ness he spoke of was a different kind of correctness than empirical truth. Meaning that orc language studies were prohibited for some reason. It didn't seem like a good idea to keep pushing the topic.

"Then I'm sure the scriptures are right," I said. "I apologize for taking your time with such pointless questions."

"Oh, no, our discussion was very worthwhile. Please tell me more about your world when you have the chance."

We parted on good terms.

It was nothing but boring days for a long while after that. Once a day, I would look in on the ceremony to make sure it was going well, not that I could actually tell. It was just about the formalities. After my inspection, I would meet with Worion and hear his report, but the reports were always the same. "Going steady. Nothing out of order."

Once every five days, I would write a similar message to be delivered to the capital.

I'd been given the job just in case something unforeseen were to happen, but perhaps also because I was seen as having too much time on my hands. This role was too boring for someone who had a proper job to do, and it would be a waste to use them here.

I had seen everything the fortress had to offer, and I itched for some fresh way to kill my remaining time there. Worion would occasionally come to see me, and I'd tell him about my world. I didn't mind talking about it, but his insatiable appetite for knowledge was exhausting. He'd always press a matter to the point where I didn't know the answer.

Take television, for example. I only knew how to operate a TV, but had no idea how it worked. Each time I spoke with someone like Worion, I would be reminded just how little I actually knew about my own world. Eventually, he realized I was no scientist, and he finally stopped asking the really deep questions.

I did make one delightful discovery at the fortress, however. After searching every nook and cranny of the place, I finally managed to find a few anthills. One of the ant tribes seemed fond of attacking the others. Even though it was winter, each day its soldiers energetically ventured out to plunder. They would win or lose their battle and return home, and I never grew tired of watching.

This day they must have won because each returned to their nest carrying a round cocoon-like trophy. The way they carried their spoils in single file made it seem like a victory parade.

"Hero...umm, are you free?"

A soldier had timidly addressed me as I stared absentmindedly at the ants. I saw he was the same one who had been my guide about the fortress.

I stood, straightening my posture to look more dignified.

"Yes, what is it?"

He looked at me dubiously, as if I were just some weirdo who stared at anthills and was now pretending to be a noble hero.

"A carriage has arrived from your territory. They have a delivery for you."

Ah, it was finally here. A while ago, I'd had one of the fortress's dragon riders deliver a letter to Kadann Hill.

"Thank you. I'll see to it at once. Where is the messenger now?"

"The main hall of the central tower, sir!"

"Understood."

I started in that direction, and trailing behind me, the soldier asked, "Erm, d-do you mind me asking what you were doing back there?"

Trying not to let my heroic bearing slip again, I answered as convincingly as I could, "It is a divination method from my hometown. The battles of the ants imitate our reality, and by watching them, I can foresee how our own conflicts will go."

"I-I see." He sounded convinced. "So, did you figure anything out?"

"Yes, that our victory is inevitable. The battle to achieve it may be harsh, but in the end we will triumph."

This was nonsense, of course, but my standing gave the lie a sense of legitimacy. Satisfied, the naïve young soldier returned to his station. Once there, he would surely spread the hero's prediction to his colleagues.

George awaited me in the main hall. He held a chain in his hand, the other end of which was connected to Johnny's collar. Johnny was a bright, well-behaved orc who would never lash out at people, but if we didn't chain him, he might be mistaken for an escaped orc and eliminated. Outside of my territory, the chain was needed for his own safety.

"Your Excellency, I've brought the goods you requested."

Orcs on Dragonbone Ridge were treated as mere livestock, hardworking beasts of burden.

"Well done. I've arranged the use of a cabin on the edge of the village. You'll stay there with Johnny for the time being."

There was a village a short distance from Dragonjaw Gate. While I called it a village, there were no farmers there, as it was a settlement where merchants gathered to cater to the needs of the soldiers. There were shops, bars, and brothels, among other things, as well as some civilian housing for those soldiers with families. It was the destination for soldiers with free time on their hands.

There had formerly been far more soldiers stationed here, but now empty houses were the village's most prominent feature. I had managed to secure one of these. This arrangement offered privacy and prevented Johnny from having to sleep with the other orcs in their dungeon cells. Not to mention, George had originally been a priest, and there was no guarantee he would go unrecognized.

My language lessons with Johnny resumed that very day. The cabin my guests stayed in was quite close to my own quarters, so I would drop by whenever I had the chance to teach Johnny the names of various new items.

At first, the lady we hired as a housekeeper was disgusted, and she kept her distance from George and Johnny. However, once I'd demonstrated Johnny's tricks to her, her attitude changed dramatically. Eventually, she even considered our clever boy cute. She was also quite warm toward George, and he reported to me that she was looking after them both with kindness.

Sometimes, soldiers on break would come to watch me train Johnny in the yard. I told them it was research to see if I could turn an orc into a soldier to fight on our side, but I could tell they saw through my façade. To them, it seemed I was just fooling around, teaching an orc tricks to kill time. To reward him for his tricks, they started throwing apples and coins whenever they watched Johnny carry out my commands. These rewards became Johnny's food and George's pocket change.

The number of soldiers dropping by to watch gradually increased. Before I knew it, George had installed benches in front of the house, and on those days when the crowd grew especially large, a local tavern would set up a stall nearby. The tavern owner would always bow to me, beaming, when we crossed paths. It seemed his stand was quite profitable.

Johnny's tricks were nothing too flashy or complicated. Everyone was just starved for entertainment. Occasionally there were hecklers, and they put Johnny off, making it harder for him to work. While I did consider driving them away, I didn't want people talking about how I was secretly sheltering an orc. I wanted these spectators to see us in a good light.

On this day I was training Johnny as usual when I heard a soft "ah" from the crowd, and all the onlookers went silent. I turned to see Worion approaching, leading a number of priests.

"I heard rumor of the hero doing some peculiar things," Worion said. "What is the meaning of this?"

I'd been dreading this. The usually gentle head scholar wore quite the grim expression. Perhaps I should have been a little more covert, but it was too late for regrets.

I started off with an excuse I already had prepared. "Our

shortage of troops has grown serious. I'm training him to see if we can repurpose captured orcs as soldiers. If we can make orcs fight other orcs, we can lower the losses of humanity." To me, this sounded perfect.

"The subjugation of orcs is the divine duty of all true believers, and true believers fight for themselves." With one stroke, he defeated me. "I took the liberty of watching this training of yours from afar."

Worion glanced at Johnny's feet, where various sorts of plants littered the ground. I had been listing the names of plants, which Johnny would then place in the order given.

"I fail to see how knowing the names of plants relates to military training." He'd already seen through the act. "Also, if you wanted to train it to be a soldier, why did you choose a female orc?"

What a shocking revelation. Johnny was actually a girl? Well, in my own defense, while orcs were perpetually naked, they didn't have dangling bits like humans did. Their sexual organs were tucked away in the folds of their bodies. Leave it to a learned man like Worion to distinguish an orc's gender in a moment.

I didn't consider myself an exceptionally intelligent man, and the exchange had a hot panic creeping up inside me. Picking up on this, Worion heaved a deep sigh.

"Hero, I see you have not given up on your ideas."

"R-right."

"I would not want you filling our virtuous adherents with such nonsense as orcs being able to understand words. I ask that you abstain from this little performance of yours."

"I-I'm sorry."

I lowered my head. I had no choice but to humble myself, if that was what it took to avoid trouble.

"The show is over!" Worion called out to the onlookers. "Be at ease... No one here is to blame. Reflect upon your faith as you fulfill your duties, but rest is also one of a soldier's duties. So disperse now, and seek your rest!"

The crowd broke up with a few glances our way, leaving just Worion, Johnny, and myself. Once we were alone, the head scholar addressed me. "Hero, it is really quite troubling for you to be doing this. It seems you and I need to have a nice long chat on the matter. I would like to invite you to dinner this evening, if you would accept."

It seemed there was a lecture in store, more than a simple chat, but for now the trouble had died down.

"Of course," I said, lowering my head again. "I'm sorry for creating a problem."

"It is fine, as long as you understand the importance of what I am saying." With a courteous bow, Worion turned and led his priests away.

That night, as invited, I joined Worion for dinner. Like me, he had been afforded a room in the barracks meant for those of noble standing. Despite this, it was still a room in a fortress, not spacious at all and bereft of decorations. With a table, two chairs, and a priest standing by to serve us, the space felt cramped. Even the food was plain. Grilled river fish as the main course, and a thin vegetable soup, rounded out with hard bread. Our glasses were filled with diluted ale.

"My apologies," Worion said. "This must seem frugal compared to what you usually dine on, but this is my customary fare."

I normally ate what the soldiers did, which was never anything extravagant, but there was usually some meat and the helpings of fish were greater. Plus, the ale wasn't diluted, and I was allowed refills if desired.

We offered our prayers, then commenced eating a quiet meal, which given the portions was over soon enough. I asked, "Do the other priests eat like this too?"

After swallowing a mouthful of bread, Worion replied, "At present, these portions wouldn't be sufficient for the others, channeling their mana all day as they do. They need to eat better than me."

"I see."

"Well, are you ready now for our little chat?"

The server left without a sound. It was finally lecture time—or so I thought, but Worion rose from his seat and began fishing through a box behind him. The item he was searching for was apparently at the very bottom. When he finally produced it, it turned out to be a wine bottle made from glass, which wasn't a common material in this world. From the tableware the server had left behind, Worion took our two wooden cups. He filled one of them to the brim with amber liquid from his bottle and placed it before me.

Our eyes met, and there was a mischievous glint in his. Poison, perhaps? No, it couldn't be. I warily brought the cup near my lips and inhaled a strong vapor that bore the scent of a distilled spirit aged in a wooden barrel. This was the first time I'd come across such a thing in this world. Even the feast in Kerulgarz hadn't supplied it. The only alcoholic beverages I'd encountered so far were ale, mead, and wine.

I took a slow sip, then nodded my approval.

"It's wonderful."

"I see you've had it before." Worion looked somewhat disappointed, as if he had hoped for me to choke at the liquor's strength. Distilled alcohol had to be a real rarity in this world.

"Yes. They have even more potent spirits back where I come from."

"I see. You really are so far ahead there. Here we call it refined holy water. Since ancient times it's been known to prevent wounds from festering. Almost a hundred years ago, a scholar found the means to produce it, but the technique has been kept a secret."

He filled his own cup.

"This refined holy water has some extraordinary properties. For instance, it's said that those who drink it are unable to lie."

I assumed the effect he mentioned was because a drunken man tended to loosen his mouth, but I wasn't sure it was only that. I watched him take a little sip himself.

"Are you sure you should be drinking that, then?"

"I'm allowed to have it during interrogations. Only those of the firmest faith are allowed—those with beliefs strong enough to triumph over the drink. Though, of course, even I would be criticized if I were to drink it in public."

Meaning these high-ranking priests enjoyed it in secret. I'd thought I was in for a scolding, but Worion seemed more gregarious than I'd expected. I knew I would have to ask what I could before the drink got to his head.

"Please tell me, is an orc understanding words really such a dangerous thing?"

Worion placed his cup down and nodded solemnly.

"Yes, such a pursuit is strictly prohibited."

"But why?"

"I do not know. I did not even know it was taboo until my predecessor committed the sin himself and was punished for it."

"So few know of the taboo despite it being such a serious matter?"

"Very few are curious enough to study those filthy beings, their language—as such—even more so. Perhaps those up top believe that spreading word of the ban would only stimulate more curiosity in these matters, even academic curiosity."

Understandable enough.

"Regardless, my predecessor continued doing his research even after being warned. He ignored these warnings until he was finally driven from the temple and had his sacred name tarnished. Publicly, he was punished for defacing a statue of God."

"What is a sacred name?"

"It is a name received upon being ordained as a priest. We are made to discard our original names. Having one's sacred name revoked would make one nameless; it is the second-harshest punishment a priest can receive, after death. It is hardly better than a death sentence. The law will not protect the nameless."

Worion took in a little more of the concoction.

"You should stop trying to learn the orcish language. If the head priest heard, even the hero could be excommunicated."

Excommunicated? The rat-priest had threatened to do just that, but honestly, it didn't bother me too much. Worion seemed to pick up on this, and went on to say, "Of course, you are the hero from another world. You would not step off the path even if our God abandoned you. However, please do not forget that it is our temple that recognizes you and guarantees your position in this world. Without our support, it would be quite hard to gain anyone's trust."

That was a strong threat, but from his expression, I could tell he was speaking from the heart.

"Thanks for the warning," I said, bowing my head. However, I had no intention of calling off my research. His kind words weren't wasted, in that they impressed on me the need to be more careful.

The intuitive head scholar sighed. "You do not plan on stopping, do you?"

I shook my head wordlessly.

Worion closed his eyes, tilted his face to the heavens, and offered a prayer. Once he had finished, he downed the rest of his cup in one gulp. He then looked me straight in the eye.

"Hero, are you able to read and write our language?"

I was a bit surprised by the sudden question. "Well, I can read, but writing is a bit...eh."

My translation ability didn't go beyond reading his language for some reason. When writing was necessary, I would have to dictate to another, though in this world it wasn't uncommon for even nobles to be unable to write. In fact, it was rare for people above a certain level of power to pick up a brush themselves.

"Then allow me to introduce you to a good teacher."

"Oh! Please do."

I didn't really get his reasons, but it was a welcome offer. It would obviously be more convenient for me if I could write on my own.

"Northwest of here, farther north than Chezarith Castle, there is a poor village called Aenidem. A desolate place, facing the sea. From there, it is two days through the mountains to the nearest temple, which is the farthest north of our places of worship. In a cave near Aenidem, there lives a hermit. At times, he teaches the local children to write in exchange for food. They call him an eccentric, but he is the best teacher I know of. Hero, why not learn writing from him?"

Chezarith? I almost doubted my ears.

The country there was enclosed by a crescent-shaped mountain ridge, open to the west. Chezarith Castle lay at its northernmost edge. According to Rigel, it was the farthest castle from the royal capital. To go beyond that point would seem like falling off the edge of the map.

"May I know the hermit's name?"

"He has none. It was taken from him."

Ah, so that was what this was about.

"He is known to be incredibly hard to get close to. Gaining his trust will be no simple matter. However, if you bring this to him, I'm sure any old man would open his heart."

With that, Worion pushed the cork back into the bottle we had been drinking from and nudged the incredibly valuable liquor toward me.

"Why are you doing this?" If only certain people were allowed to partake of this refined holy water, he was encouraging me to commit taboo. How could someone of his position do such a thing?

"Watching you play with orcs reminded me of my predecessor. My master." I didn't consider my studies "playing," but I didn't interrupt him. "Like you, my master also sought to communicate with an orc. He was quite a clever orc, but he was killed when my master was exiled. A waste, in my opinion."

Worion's eyes, bloodshot from drink, peered deeply into mine.

"I presume you do not want to learn orcish purely for the sake of knowledge. You hope to change something."

He made swirling motions with his cup, but it was empty. His eyes roamed the table, starved until they spotted my cup. He reached out, took it, and downed its contents too.

"I do not know *what* you're trying to change, Hero, but there is one thing I do know. Those above me closed off the path to knowledge, and they drove out my master because they feared change."

His face had flushed red, the extra drink hitting him hard.

"Walling up truth and knowledge is against the very duty of scholars! Could there be anything more frustrating, more humiliating? I have no power or courage to oppose them, so you will have to overcome them for me. You will have to take my revenge."

"I don't know if I can fulfill your expectations, but I won't waste this opportunity you've afforded me."

Worion seemed satisfied enough with my answer. After a nod, he slumped forward in his seat. He was not a heavy drinker, evidently, and had pushed himself, perhaps to gain the courage to reveal what he had.

The conversation was over. I stood, turned away, and reached for the doorknob, but I paused when I heard Worion mumbling behind me.

"Hero... If you can...please protect him. The law no longer does, and he has little left to his name. Please... My master... My friend."

Then he fell silent, except for the deep breathing of slumber.

PLANET OF THE ORCS

CHAPTER 5

THE HERMIT AND THE CAVE

STRADDLING VERALGON, I made my way to Chezarith Castle.

The castle was positioned at the northwestern tip of the crescent-shaped territory. In summer, it would apparently be possible to reach there in two days, but the dragon riders I consulted told me it would take five at this time of year. In summer, one could simply fly directly over the ocean, but with the days shorter during the winter months, the sun would set somewhere in the middle of the journey. Flying over a pitch-black sea was hazardous to all but the most seasoned veterans. Therefore, I needed to take a detour along the coast.

I'd received His Majesty's permission to take a temporary leave from Dragonjaw Gate. I couldn't reveal I was searching for some hermit in the mountains, so I instead wrote, *"As a dragon rider, I would like to acquire more experience flying long distances."* The king himself responded, first apologizing for delegating such a tedious job to me. Then, he gave me permission to take it easy for a while. It seemed he thought I had grown weary of the boring ceremony and wanted to break up the monotony.

He concluded his message with something along the lines of, *"Do not take on any unnecessary tasks in your travels, even if someone begs you to assist them in some matter. If such a request occurs, send the information to the palace."* Well, I didn't want any headaches either. If I could throw a request like that to someone else, I would certainly do so.

The dragon keeper who'd brought me the message said he would accompany me to Chezarith, per His Majesty's orders. The boy-king really was good at looking after people.

It was fine weather all the way. Without a cloud in the sky, an updraft was all it took to climb high above the world. The wind was cold enough, but compared to those icy winds from when I had crossed the Dragonbone Ridge, it felt like a light breeze. The dragon keeper riding behind me gave me tips on how to use strong upward air currents coming off cliffs and the sea to gain altitude.

Clinging fast to my back, his stubble scraping against my ears, the keeper instructed, "Okay, a little closer to the cliffs! Position his head a bit more downwind! Wonderful! Now you've got it!"

With his help, I learned better how to use the terrain to my advantage, especially when sustaining a flight of a long distance. Perhaps if I'd had this knowledge earlier, I could have crossed the Dragonbone Ridge with less fatigue.

He cried, "Pardon my saying so, but it is funny how you handle a dragon so well yet you know so little about using the wind!"

"I never! Learned to fly! In my! Homeland!"

If we didn't scream into each other's ears, the roar of the wind would blow our words away. The dragon keeper seemed more accustomed to talking like this, and he spoke with a particular cadence. His voice came through well, despite the wind.

"Really? I was convinced you kept dragons in your homeland!"

Definitely not. There would be quite a scene, were I to fly a dragon there.

He went on, "I guess dragon riding really comes down to the talent!"

"Well you sound! Pretty knowledgeable! About air currents!"

"I've been riding behind dragon riders for thirty years now!"

The veteran dragon keeper related how he had banged on the army's gates, hoping to become a rider. However, he lacked the natural talent to pull it off.

"But hey, once you get used to it, being a dragon keeper ain't so bad! I still get to fly, don't I? And it's a lot safer!" He laughed into the wind.

In the evening, three days out from Dragonjaw Gate, we arrived in the airspace above Chezarith Castle. The weather had been on our side, and having put the keeper's tricks into play, we arrived considerably earlier than scheduled.

The castle was built atop a cliff at the tip of a long and narrow peninsula. The base of the cliff had been eroded by waves, the castle above practically suspended in the air. As the castle had been built on such a narrow plot of land, it was tall and elongated, looking terribly unstable, as if a gust of wind were all it would take for it to topple into the sea.

After one circle around the castle, I continued on my course north. A short distance beyond was a large port town, where the lord had permitted the dragon riders to build their own dragon house. It was the third largest such building after the grand dragon house and the facility in Dragonjaw Gate. The plan was to leave Veralgon there, spend a night, and visit the lord of the castle the next morning. There could be trouble if I loitered around someone's territory without permission, so I would need to speak with the lord first before going in search of the hermit.

As I was unloading Veralgon at the dragon house, a messenger with a long and well-groomed white beard sought me out and courteously lowered his head.

"I take it this white dragon belongs to the hero from another world. My name is Bangas, son of Bangel. I am a knight in service to the Lord of Chezarith. My lord wishes to invite the hero to tonight's feast. I know you must be tired from your trip, but won't you accompany me to the castle?"

I'd intended to go anyway, so this invitation just made things easier.

"I humbly accept the invitation. I was meaning to drop by."

"Wonderful," Bangas said, smiling. "I have a horse waiting; I shall guide you there. Please just call out once you're ready. The one who accompanied you is invited as well, of course."

"Come back as soon as you can, Hero," the dragon keeper, who had to remain with Veralgon, anxiously urged me before I headed off to Chezarith Castle. Veralgon was in a bad mood, but then again, when wasn't he?

It was around thirty minutes from the port town to the castle by horse. While the castle had looked precarious from above, it reared quite splendidly when seen from below. In fact, it was nearly impregnable, with no clear angle of attack. On three sides, high cliffs loomed above the sea, sheltering it from ship and dragon, and the only ground route was that narrow peninsula with its treacherous road. It would be all but impossible to install siege weapons upon it.

Bangas's call was answered by the rattling of chains as the sturdy gate rose. Beyond the threshold stood a familiar man.

"Hero! We lived another day, thanks to you. You have my gratitude!"

This man, along with the twenty behind him, got down on one knee and lowered his head. There was no mistaking the scar on his face. He was Galeom, the one who had saved me and Kyel when we were shot down over an orc village. Back then, he had introduced himself as some lord, though I didn't quite remember the details.

Having been abandoned in orcish territory with his men, he'd entrusted me with a letter that detailed instructions for a rescue ship. I was safely recovered by Sir Rigel's rescue party, and upon my return, I made sure the letter was delivered to his territory. It appeared the message had been safely received.

"I simply handed off a letter. In fact, I'm the one indebted to *you*. Please, raise your head."

Galeom looked up and reached out his hand. "Hero, give us the honor of exchanging the vows of comrades, that our debts shall always be equal."

Had he learned of my status after he'd returned here? His tone had changed, as if he were addressing someone above him. I grabbed his hand and pulled him to his feet. Cheers erupted behind him. On closer inspection, I vaguely remembered his surviving knights as well. I shook their hands and shared hugs with them too.

"Now we are comrades in war!" Galeom cried, and together we hurried toward the promised feast.

Barrels of ale were piled in the four corners of the room, and extravagant food covered four long tables arranged into a square. In the center of the square blazed a fire pit, over which a plump pig was being roasted whole. I was surprised they had managed to prepare all this in the short time since learning of my arrival. The ale had simply been brought up from the cellar, but the cooks must have gone through hell.

In front of the fire, surrounded by the banquet tables, a minstrel performed a song based on my fall and crash, and the battle that had followed. Galeom had had his personal poet draft it upon returning to his territory alive.

The story detailed in the ballad was this:

Galeom had led the army of Chezarith Castle through Dragonjaw Gate to overrun the orcs, taking out one force of orcish resistance after the next and reaping the spoils of war. However, those cowardly orcs sealed the entrance to the valley, and Galeom's men could no longer return home. The hero summoned here from another world led the dragon riders to breach the orcs' blockade. Unfortunately, even the dragon riders were no match for the enemy formations, and at the end of an intense battle, the hero and a young dragon rider were shot out of the sky. Unwilling to abandon his injured friend, the hero elected to remain in the enemy's midst, resulting in him being assailed by over ten thousand orcs at once.

Meanwhile, Galeom and his men had seen the dragons fall from the sky, and they rushed to the aid of the two riders. There, they witnessed the hero protecting his friend as orcish corpses piled around him like castle ramparts. Ultimately, though, the hero ran out of strength and collapsed to his knees. Without a moment to lose, Galeom blew his horn and ordered a charge. Despite being ten thousand strong, the orcish army fell into a panic at the sudden appearance of an army bearing down on them, and the knights of Chezarith tore through their ranks to rescue the hero. Afterward, when the hero was taken away by dragon, Galeom entrusted him with a letter requesting that help be sent. Then, Galeom and his men marched west toward the sea, crushing orcish platoons along the way. However, a fearsome foe pursued them: the beak-dogs led by the infamous Black Dog.

The fleet Galeom had requested in his letter arrived just in time, and the Black Dog was left stamping his feet in frustration as the humans made off with their spoils.

The rambling song was nonsense, to be honest. Nevertheless, the minstrel was showered with applause for his glorious recitation.

The general summary was correct, but all the accomplishments of battle had been greatly overblown. I didn't remember any hero forming a mountain of corpses, nor even going up against ten thousand orcs. All I'd ever cut down there were dogs.

On top of all this, every single knight who had taken part was given their own dramatic scene, making the whole ballad seem endless. Each participant had at least one line, with a whole stanza dedicated to those who'd contributed most notably. Apparently, each and every fighter had taken down between ten and twenty orcs on their own. Meanwhile, as I recalled, there had only been about two hundred orcs opposing us in total.

Despite how ridiculous the ballad was, those who had survived that scene cheered in excitement. Torturously, the minstrel was made to repeat the same song over and over, smiling as he fulfilled the men's calls for encores. The tray beside him piled higher and higher with silver and copper coins upon every repetition.

It would have been rude of me to speak out about it. Anyway, it was through the song that I learned what had happened to these men after we parted. Though they had ultimately prevailed, it had not been an easy journey, a number of them having died along the way.

The minstrel finished the song yet again. In high spirits, Galeom dug out a silver coin and threw it at the pile. A few other coins scattered at the impact, but the minstrel paid it no mind. He had earned so much, he didn't care about a little lost change.

When he was back in his seat, Galeom turned toward me. "You don't have to be a stranger, Hero. If you'd told me in advance you were coming, I'd have prepared something better. Unfortunately, quite a few of our men are away on a bit of business today. I'm sure they'd be saddened to know they missed you."

"Sorry about that. I didn't mean to be rude by just appearing like this, but, truth be told, I'm here on urgent business."

"Oh, some important mission, then?"

"Yes. I heard I could find a hermit here who was exiled from the temple."

"I see! You came to take him in!"

"Not exactly. He was originally a scholar, and I need to borrow his wisdom."

"Wisdom, eh? What sort of information are you after?"

This was where things could get dicey.

"I was told to keep that part a secret. I hope you understand."

"Very well. I'll lend you some troops. Having locals with you would definitely help in a missing person search."

"Please, that's not necessary. I already know the general location, and I travel by dragon. I'd be thankful, though, if I could have official permission to search."

"Hmm..."

After staring pensively at the ceiling for a moment, Galeom returned his gaze to me.

"I'll write you up a letter, then. You won't be suspected of any suspicious activity if you have me vouching for you."

"Thank you."

"Where is this hermit of yours hiding, anyway?"

"Near a village called Aenidem, apparently."

"Aenidem?" Galeom furrowed his brow. A nervous-looking man beside him whispered something in his ear.

"Oh, there? Quite a remote place, that."

Even more remote than this remote region? Impressive.

"I'll have my man here draw up a simple map for you. It's a tiny place. You could try asking someone for directions, but I doubt you'd find anyone who knows where it is."

"Seriously, thank you for everything."

"It's no trouble. We've exchanged the vows of comrades, after all!" Galeom threw back his head and laughed happily.

Then I enjoyed another three repetitions of that song, and a fair bit of alcohol to make it more endurable. Later, with the letter of permission and map in hand, I returned to the dragon house at the port.

Thanks to Galeom's map, I managed to arrive at Aenidem without difficulty. It lay in a valley in the depths of a jagged coastline. There was a small, stony beach lined with numerous banged-up boats that I suspected were no longer seaworthy. Facing the beach and running up the slope of the valley was a clump of around ten ramshackle cottages. They were so battered, in fact, that I would consider the orc shed at Kadann Hill a welcome improvement. This place seemed terribly poor, and was smaller than anticipated.

Fighting against the gusts of wind blowing off the cove, I finally managed to lower my dragon onto the slender stretch of beach. The dragon rider who had followed me gave up on touching down with his own dragon, and instead remained circling overhead.

I dismounted and looked around, but there wasn't a soul to be seen. Perhaps the place had already been abandoned? But no, that couldn't be true. From on high, I had seen smoke coming from one of the houses. Surely someone still lived here. They were most likely just wary of these strangers with dragons. I would have to be the one to initiate contact.

I handed Veralgon's reins off to the keeper, then turned my feet toward the nearest hut.

As I approached, I noticed the door was open ever so slightly, with two pairs of eyes showing in the gap, one set above the other. Judging by their low positions, they likely belonged to children. Perfect. Since the hermit taught kids how to read, they'd be the best bet for guiding me to him.

"Hello there," I called, smiling.

The eyes withdrew, and someone slammed the door shut. The slender arm I'd glimpsed likely belonged to their mother. Undaunted, I continued to the door and knocked on it. There was no response.

I knocked again and this time spoke.

"I'm sorry for startling you—I don't mean any harm. There's something I'd like to ask, if you can spare a moment."

There was still no response. What now? The door didn't appear to be locked, so I could just open it to look inside, but I didn't want to alarm them. Perhaps I was better off giving up and trying another house. I was starting for the next one over when a child's voice called after me.

"Mistah, are you the hewo?"

I turned just in time to see a small boy dragged back into the house.

"Shh! I told you to keep quiet!" I heard an adult woman scold him in a whisper. I took care to sound as affable as possible when I called out again.

"Oh, so you are home. Trust me, I'm no one to fear. As you can see, I have a permit from the lord."

I took out Galeom's parchment and unfurled it. The door cracked open again, and a haggard woman's face was framed in the gap.

"From our lord, eh? Well, unfortunately I can't read. You should try asking the chief."

She pointed to a decrepit hut only a little larger than her own, then began shutting her door again. Before she could, however, that small boy poked his head out. When the door slammed on him, he groaned, fighting against his mother's attempts to drag him back.

"I can wead! Show me!"

"Go right ahead. Look here."

I showed him the paper.

"Err... *'Th-this man is the h-hewo sum...summoned from a-anodder world.'* It says he's the hewo! I knew it!"

At that exclamation, another boy around three years older popped his head out.

"Hey, hey! Let me see too!"

This kid pushed his younger brother's head out of the way, and scanned the parchment paper. It was his turn to read aloud.

"*'This man is the hero summoned from another world, and my comrade-in-arms. He searches for the...hermit?...of the cave. I ask that everyone in my territory do what they can to assist him.'*"

Having finished reading, the boy's eyes opened wide. Their mother seemed bewildered, unable to catch up with what was going on.

"It has the lord's crest too! He really is the hero!"

"I toad you! He wode a white dwagon!"

The brothers jumped in excitement, but their mother went pale. It seemed rumors about me had reached even these far-flung settlements.

"What is the hewo here fow?" the younger one asked me.

The older one immediately scolded him. "Stupid, it says right here. He wants the hermit of the cave!"

"What's a hewmit ovacave?"

The older boy didn't have an answer for that.

"I came here to find an old man who lives in one of the nearby caves," I replied gently.

"Oh, I know him! You want Old Man Badjah—mmph!"

The older brother clapped a hand over the younger one's mouth. The man who had once been the keeper of all the temple's knowledge, in the role of chief scholar, now apparently went by the nickname Old Man Badger.

"Shh! He told us not to tell anyone!"

The boy thought he was whispering, but I could hear everything. The mother looked between the letter and her children, more confused than ever. In any case, it seemed Old Man Badger was liked well enough around here for these boys to want to protect him.

I spoke in a tone so placating it disgusted even me. "I came to borrow his knowledge. I won't do anything bad to him."

"You got pwoof?" the smaller one snarled. What a brave child he was. I hoped he carried that quality into adulthood.

Well, what evidence *did* I have? I placed my bag down and fished through it.

"Look, I brought a present for him," I said, and I held up the bottle of liquor. I didn't expect them to understand its value, but the simple fact that the bottle was made of glass would hopefully make an impression.

"What's that?" The kids looked at me dubiously. The meaning wasn't getting through. Well, they were children, after all.

"It's ale," I explained, as there was no easy way to describe "refined holy water."

The doubt suddenly disappeared from their eyes.

"Oh, ale."

"Yeah, ale."

"He does like his drink," said the older boy.

Looking at each other, the brothers obviously reached an agreement.

"All right, Hero! Follow us!"

The two young boys bolted from the house, taking off toward the mountains.

"Ah! W-wait!" their mother cried, but they didn't even look back.

I bowed to the mother, then followed them.

Children really were rowdy, no matter the world. Despite their heavy panting, the boys raced up the steep slope behind the houses, their pace barely slacking. Were they not cold, dressed in their frayed and patchworked clothing? I myself was cold, even in my dragon rider's flight suit.

"Over here!" one of them called to me from the top of a hill.

I caught up to find them standing under a great tree, a mat nailed into its trunk. The elder brother lifted the mat aside and shouted, "Old Man Badger! You have a visitor!"

So this hollow tree was the hermit's so-called cave? Certainly not what I'd imagined. Perhaps a bear had once dug out this space to use for hibernation.

"If you don't come out, we'll smoke you out!" the kids screamed, and they began clacking rocks together, as if to strike a spark and start a fire. Oh, such little brats. This was how they treated their benefactor, who'd taught them the written word?

From inside a voice growled, "Shut up! I heard you, goddammit!"

The mat was flipped open. The old man who lurched out was just skin and bones, his hair wispy vestiges. The sack-like garment he wore could hardly be called clothing, and it just barely covered him.

"Run away!" the kids screamed, and they raced down the slope.

"Of course it's Ciel's brats again!" the old man grumbled. "Just when I was getting comfortable! Go away, brats! Don't come again!"

Seeing the old man shake his fist and scream after them, the fleeing kids stopped below to look back and chuckle.

"Old Man Badger," they yelled, "you have a guest!"

"I told you not to bring anyone!"

"He's the hero!"

"Don't be stupid! This man's blowing smoke up your ass!"

"It's true! He has a white dragon!"

"A white... Veralgon? It can't be..."

It was then that the old man finally registered me.

"So you're the hero who the temple called here?"

"For what it's worth."

The old man glared at me. His forceful, terrifying eyes seemed completely unsuited to his frail body, which looked to be on the brink of death.

"What's the temple's hero got to do with me? Did you come to arrest me?"

An ominous brand stood out on the man's forehead—the mark of exile. Those who had been branded could no longer receive any protection under the law.

"I'm here to—"

"Yeah, I can tell... I'm not an idiot. Oi! You kids! Go home already!"

The kids had sneaked closer again, but the old man shooed them away. This time, the boys seemed to sense they were pushing him too far, and they turned back toward the village below.

"I get it," he continued. "You wouldn't have come on the dragon if you wanted to take me in. I can't ride on them. So, you're going to kill me on the spot."

"No, just listen—"

"Then what is it? I've done as they ordered—I've stopped all my research into orcs! I haven't written any of their words, and I haven't even snorted my nose! What more could you want?"

"I'm telling you, I'm not here to punish—"

"For God's sake, quit beating around the bush! Out with it, already!"

I sighed, then said, "I came to borrow your wisdom."

"Wisdom? Ask the scholars, then. I left all the fruits of my research behind. No need to find me... You should be able to understand my work as long as you read the documents. Or can you not read?"

"I can read, but all your documents are long gone."

When I said this, his eyes filled with suspicion.

"You really love beating around the bush. You plan to drag a confession out of me, then kill me! Ah, but there's really no need for a confession, is there? Just kill a nameless old man, and no questions will be asked. Who's to know? I'm sure Romwell has already told you all about me, anyway—that halfwit. Such an untrustworthy coward, and yet he's so fixated on notions of loyalty. That's why he won't kill me, so long as I keep my word. How's someone supposed to live like that, eh?"

I simply couldn't follow his rambling rant. Who even was Romwell? Could that be the name of the rat-faced head priest? Considering this man's circumstances, I couldn't blame him for doubting me. I had an idea, though, about how I might gain some trust. I held up the glass bottle Worion had given me, and the hermit's rant abruptly halted.

"This was entrusted to me by a certain high-ranking priest. Please, take it."

"Th-this is..."

He snatched the bottle from my hands, popped the cork, and took a good whiff. Then, he resealed it with shaking hands, and glared at me again.

"Do you know what this is?"

"It's distilled alcohol. I heard it's valuable. I sampled one sip when it was given to me."

"You fool! This is no ordinary spirit. This is from the first ten barrels Saint Horun ever brewed."

"Who's that?"

"You tasted it without even knowing who Saint Horun is? Your ignorance is staggering! You should be ashamed of yourself! Well then, listen up. Saint Horun was the name of the scholar who devised a way to distill this drink from ale. The contents of this bottle were made using his perfected technique, which means it has been over eighty years since this noble holy water was made. I know for a fact seven barrels had run dry before I came here, and I doubt even half of the rest remains. The barrels don't leak, but for some reason the liquid in them disappears bit by bit over time. I'm sure God is stealing it. Yes, I'm sure God is a terrible drunkard. If he weren't, he wouldn't have shaped the world so crudely!"

I couldn't get a word in. Had this gift not been to my advantage, after all?

"Oi, the guy who gave it to you... No, don't say it. It was Worion, wasn't it? Good grief, I used to think he was smart, but he turned out to be a fool. He should have savored this on his own, for however many years it lasted. Does he not understand it won't last a night if he gives it to me? And you, don't you find it strange? A priest as noble as I was, exiled for supposedly defacing a statue of God's while in a drunken stupor? What idiotic charges, but no one dared question it. Worion knew the circumstances, and even he went along with it. Who do you think I am? But first of all—"

His words suddenly ceased, and he held his hand out to me...a filthy appendage covered in dirt and grime. I reached out to shake it, only for him to smack my hand away.

"No, you creep! I'm telling you to get me a cup! Or do you want this poor old man to drink straight from the bottle? I get it... You really are here to kill me!"

"I'm *not*. Give me a moment and I'll find a cup."

I rummaged through my bag but came up empty-handed. The cup I'd thought I had must be with the camping gear I'd left at the dragon house.

Left with little choice, I picked up a nearby stone around the size of my fist, while the old man watched me curiously. Holding the stone in my left hand, I projected a knife-sized spear of light from my right hand. A spear of light could cut almost anything, and with it, I hollowed out the rock into a cup. It was crudely shaped, but beggars can't be choosers.

The old man's eyes widened. "Huh...you can project a spear without using any magical implements."

I was happy for the opportunity to demonstrate my hero's special abilities. Maybe now I'd earned a little respect?

"Romwell must like you quite a bit."

Hm? What did that mean?

"What's with that face? He never told you? The art of wielding magic without the use of blessed equipment is only passed down to a select few of the Knights Templar. It's not too difficult, once you know the trick, which is precisely why it's only taught to those who have sworn absolute loyalty to the temple and proven their devotion. If just anyone who possesses mana could use magic without tools, the temple would lose much of its reason to even exist. The nobility would be outraged."

I'd never heard about any of this.

I said, "This ability wasn't given to me by the temple. When I was summoned to this world, God gave me the gift of mimicking any magic I witnessed."

The old man's eyes lit up.

"What an ability! Oh, I'd love to research it. So how do you go about copying magic? In the first place, how does that..." He suddenly quieted down again, his body appearing to wilt. "Eh, it's impossible for me to research now. Anyway, it's absurd. God gave you the ability to imitate magic? It would be more believable to just admit Romwell entrusted you with the skill. I can see you really are the hero, however, so what does the hero need from this sinful priest?"

I could finally get to the main point. What a long journey!

"I want to borrow your wisdom. Please teach me the language of the orcs."

The hermit gave a scornful laugh. "I see. And what would you do once you learned it?"

How was I supposed to answer that? Honesty was probably the best policy.

"I intend to negotiate with them, and hopefully achieve peace."

The exiled scholar stared at me blankly for a moment, then clutched his stomach as he burst into laughter.

"What's so funny about that?"

He ignored me, now dropping to the ground to roll in laughter. Once he had laughed to his satisfaction, he staggered back to his feet and said, "I'm not laughing at you. It's nice to dream big, kid. It looks like this is going to go just as Romwell feared."

"You mean the head priest?"

"When he censured me for my research, I brought up numerous benefits of knowing the orc language. We could get all sorts of information out of the ones we'd captured. We could hear about the state of their country—I don't even have to explain the military advantage of that. And most importantly, the orcs are clearly far more advanced when it comes to technology. I assume they discovered that knowledge in the ancient ruins. The majority of those are beyond the mountains, after all. If we could piece together all this information, we'd be fighting with an advantage."

He made absolute sense. I myself didn't see any reason to counter his views.

"Is it that serious to commit religious taboo?"

"That, a taboo? Hardly. It was just Romwell's decision. He saw things differently than I did." He shrugged. "I brought up so many advantages, and he insisted the risk was higher. I asked, why overlook all the benefits for fear of nonexistent risks? I assured him no idiot would think to use this valuable knowledge frivolously!"

He grinned at me.

"Ah, but now that idiot has come. Dear me. It turns out Romwell was right."

"Peace is a risk? What are you saying?"

"Ask him to explain his shortsighted logic. If you really plan on pursuing peace, you'll have to ask him these questions eventually. I've had to wash my hands of it. But you say you want to learn orcish, do you?"

"I do."

"Fine, then... I'll teach you. With conditions."

"Let's hear them."

"First, I want you to take me under your protection and ensure my needs are met. You have quite a bit of status, obviously. You should be able to see that one pitiful old man gets fed."

"Understood. Kadann Hill will offer you a safe haven. I promise you a room at the manor."

I'd already intended to offer this, but not just for his benefit. I didn't want to have to commute here every time I wanted a lesson from him.

"You were appointed as field marshal, then? You don't look the part at all. Be that as it may, now for condition two."

"Go on."

"You will assist my in research. First, on orcish language. My dictionary is far from complete. However, you'll have to keep my research a secret."

"And your promise with the head priest?" I asked.

"I never exactly promised not to *research*. He was more concerned with me utilizing the research. His precise phrasing was: 'If you pursue the orcish language any further in order to teach it to others, I will have you killed. So long as you refrain, I will leave you be.' If he fails to fulfill his side of that promise, that's on him."

Brave words, but I'd be the one standing between the two of them if it came to that. I really wanted him to resume his research, though, so I'd just have to keep him out of sight as best as I could.

"Very well. I'll support your research in whatever way I can."

"Then we have an agreement. I'll begin instructing you as soon as we reach your manor."

Having said this, the old man started for his hole, but he paused to turn back to me.

He said, "To tell you the truth, living here free from worldly concerns wasn't so bad. But at this age, I'm feeling the weather in my bones." To demonstrate, he stretched out his arms with a groan.

"I can see that. But tell me, why are you so fixated on the orcish language? You wouldn't be here if you'd just given up and worked on something else."

The man snorted at this question. "Like hell I could give up! Learning their language was the shortest route I could take. All the other paths would be far more troublesome. Without my efforts, there wouldn't have been any progress in my lifetime."

"Orcish is a shortcut? To what?"

"I'll explain it so even an idiot like you can understand. The true subject of my research was the technology left by the ancients."

"The people who built the grand dragon house and Dragonjaw Gate?"

"Don't interrupt! Dragonjaw Gate, yes, but not the grand dragon house. That was yet another civilization, with different technology," he huffed impatiently. "I had a dream of reviving the technology of the ancients, and restoring to humanity their level of prosperity."

"What's that got to do with the orcs?"

"Shut up and wait for me to get to that! You don't have to jump in every time your fatuous brain spasms! If you don't understand, save your questions for the end!"

Jeez, sorry.

"The ancients did not leave much. Within our territory, we only have Dragonjaw Gate, so the other scholars and I would spend our days piecing together the circle under the gate.

Of course, we hardly made any progress. One day, though, when despair was beginning to get the better of me, a dragon rider came to us with something amazing. What do you think it was?"

"I don't know."

"A book. A book written by the ancients! Some outrageous idiot named Rigel had found it. He'd flown all the way to the old capital simply out of boredom...flown straight into orc territory on an idle whim! See what I mean by outrageous idiot? Never before had I been so thankful to God for bringing idiots into the world. I was ready to apologize for all the times I'd cursed in His name."

This was some talk from a former priest. Anyway, Rigel was really getting blasted for someone who'd discovered such a valuable artifact.

"And what do you know? Of all things, that book was about Dragonjaw Gate! Not that I could read a word of it. I had to guess context from the illustrations, but there was no doubt about the subject matter. The book contained many descriptions of Dragonjaw Gate, including a complex diagram of the magic circle. I had no idea how anyone could draw up something so elaborate. It took a magnifying glass to observe the finer details. Do you know about magnifying glasses? You do? So what do you think it was? No, not the glass! I mean the *gate*."

Undeterred, he continued, "Anyway, Dragonjaw Gate is not just a fortress. There's a possibility that a massive dragon was once sealed beneath it. That's what was pictured: a dragon pinned to the ground with eight stakes. Yes, I understand your disbelief; it's written all over your face. Of course, it's possible the illustration was just a metaphor to represent something else entirely. However, based on how precisely the dragon was portrayed, and the details on a magic circle that appeared to be a binding seal, it's not out of the question. It's possible that what we call ley lines are actually—"

I felt he was getting off track.

"Um, could we get back to the—"

"What, is that how you ask someone to teach you? Teacher is feeling enthusiastic right now, so just shut up and listen! You seriously lack respect. Anyway, where were we?"

Despite his foul manner, he did return to the topic.

"There was no doubt that the book's text was crammed full of information that would help elucidate the magic circle. Decrypting that text became the central focus of my research. I started by comparing the magic circles I knew to the drawings in the book, and guessing what might be written about them. I made a little progress, just enough to work out some of the circle's functions. However, there my studies reached a dead end. I could not actually read the words themselves, so the book itself wasn't enough. What would you have done then?"

"Search in Dragonjaw Gate, perhaps?"

"That's right. Though it had been searched before, I obsessively investigated every nook and cranny. And while I did uncover a few secret rooms, I found little else. Then what next?"

"How about searching for other ruins?"

"That would be a good idea, but we know there are no other ancient ruins on our side of the mountains. Therefore, I set my sights beyond the mountains."

"Into orcish territory?"

"That's right. I talked my way into an invading force, as their chaplain, and searched the other side. Unfortunately, there weren't any ruins near the far side of the mountains. Perhaps that had been a frontier region to the ancients. No doubt there was more to be found to the south, but I could not venture that deeply into orc territory. I needed to gather information from the orcs themselves, my best bet being for them to guide me. It's obvious the orcs have investigated ancient ruins. I hoped to view whatever documents they might have written about their findings."

"I see. So that's why learning orcish was necessary."

"You finally understand? Good grief, could you be any slower?" His words were sharp, but he seemed to be enjoying himself.

"Well, look, I need to return to Dragonjaw Gate for now. I'll send someone for you as soon as I can. Please be patient."

"Fine. I just hope I don't freeze before they get here. Wait, you said Dragonjaw Gate? You're allowed to come and go as you please? What about the underground chamber?"

"I am, and the chamber is open. They're in the middle of a ceremony to reactivate the barriers, right now."

"By God! I didn't think they'd actually do it. Is it going well so far?"

"So far."

"Who's in charge?"

"Worion, the head scholar."

"I see... So he succeeded me. He's quite an idiot himself, but he's one of the better ones. He should be able to handle whatever happens."

Being a better idiot was probably the best compliment the old hermit could give.

"Since you're going to Dragonjaw Gate, then, I have one request."

CHAPTER 6

ORCS AND WORDS

THE WALLS OF THE CHAMBER that housed the massive magic circle were lined with twenty doors, spaced at regular intervals. These connected to rooms of various sizes, all of which presently served as break rooms for the priests. Long tables and many chairs had been brought into the largest of these rooms, so that it might function as a dining hall. Day and night, weary priests shuffled in, stuffed their faces, and left. Not a word would be spoken. In order to make food available at all times, the fortress's kitchen worked around the clock.

At the back of the impromptu dining hall was a marble statue, so lifelike it looked like it might start moving at any second. The male figure's features, attire, and accoutrements were carved in intricate detail, even giving a sense of the muscles beneath the cloth. Around his wrists were thirteen gold bands, making it clear he was someone of high standing. His belt buckle was shaped like the water dragon on the fortress's sluice gate. The statue's pedestal was blank, the man's name lost to history. Perhaps when the statue had been carved, the man had been so well known there hadn't seemed a need to label him. Now, though, the faded and peeling remnants of pigments only told a tale of glory long gone.

Behind the statue's pedestal, a square panel was fitted into the wall where one of the many stone blocks had once been. Removing the panel revealed a tunnel so tight that an adult would barely be able to pass through it. This narrow passage went on too far for the feeble light of a lantern to illuminate its depth.

It took quite a bit of courage for me to enter it. If I were to get wedged inside or caught on something, trapped immobile in the darkness, my life would end in a drawn-out nightmare. I wished I had brought George with me, so that I could have tied a rope to myself and told him to haul me out if something went wrong.

Bringing him along would have been too risky, though. With all the priests gathered for the ceremony, the chance that someone might recognize him greatly increased. I wanted this endeavor to go unnoticed.

I looked around the room surreptitiously. Silent priests with haggard faces were bent over their humble meals, none of them seeming to pay me any mind. I found my resolve and slipped into the tunnel.

To my relief, I found the passage slowly widened the farther I crawled. Eventually, the ceiling was high enough for me to walk with a stoop. I pressed on, lighting my way with my lantern. The air was damp, reeking of mold. Occasionally, the plop of a water droplet would break the grim silence. After a few corners, I came to a chamber no larger than the interior of a shed.

On the far wall was a relief of a human face that reminded me of the Bocca della Verità from my own world. The inside of the uncanny face's wide-open mouth was pitch-black, impenetrable even with the aid of my lantern. Tentatively, I inserted the tips of my fingers into the mouth and saw them immediately swallowed in what seemed to be a black mist. It was just as the sage had told me: this room was the work of the ancients with their magic.

This was one of the hidden rooms the scholars had found in their investigations of Dragonjaw Gate. "Finding No. 33, Chamber of the Dark God," according to their reports, but nothing else had been noted besides this ominous piece of art. However, the room possessed one more secret that hadn't been reported.

I stuck my entire arm into the hole, all the way up to the shoulder. Like the statue blocking the tunnel, the carving looked as if it were about to spring to life. Perhaps my arm would be bitten off. I held my fear in check and groped around within, my fingertips encountering a smooth sensation. Here it was: a stone sphere. After a bit more blind groping, I fitted the sphere in the palm of my hand, and then poured my mana into it.

As I did this, that black mist poured out of the relief's mouth, and I lost my vision.

"Don't panic, and don't let go," the sage had advised me. "If you do, you'll be left behind in the dark, and you'll never come back."

He'd laughed when he'd said this, but his eyes had remained serious. I didn't know if he'd just been teasing me, but I didn't feel like finding out. After I'd poured forth quite a bit of mana, the inky mist began to thin out. It wasn't too long before my vision returned, and once I could see again, the scenery had changed entirely.

"Since you're going to Dragonjaw Gate, then, I have one request."

"If it's within my power."

"Before I was exiled, I left my notes there."

"Your notes? Why?"

"Fool! Don't you get it? It's my orcish dictionary. If I hadn't concealed it, they would have burned it, so I hid away the copy that I had Potato make."

"Potato?" I asked, confused.

"The name of the orc I kept! He loved steamed potatoes, okay? You don't need to pick at every insignificant detail. Good grief, the time wasted in talking with fools!"

How was I not supposed to question a potato copying a dictionary?

"When I was a young scholar, my superiors always shoved dull research topics on me. Later, when I was advanced enough to choose my own research, my subordinates would come to me for help with their own dull pursuits. I discovered the hidden room's secret around the time that I'd become fed up with it all. Instead of reporting my findings, I used the room as a hideout whenever idiots were looking for me."

He then described to me where to find the entrance to the secret room, and what to do once there. Before I parted ways with the hermit, that exiled priest, I asked him what name I should address with him going forward.

"I am all out of names. I shed my birth name when I became a priest, and my priestly name was stripped from me."

"Then I'll call you 'the sage.'"

The sage snorted. "Whatever."

It was then that I left him, and soon enough I was steering Veralgon back to Dragonjaw Gate.

With the mist cleared, I saw I was in a completely different place from before. I removed my hand from the inky blackness of the dark god's mouth, and sighed when I confirmed it was still in one piece.

The passageway through which I had entered the secret room was gone, and I now found myself standing in a larger chamber with a high ceiling. The first thing I noticed when I turned from the face on the wall was a well-lit stone bed. An ancient skeleton lay upon this faceup. Nearly all of its clothing had fallen into meager scraps, though various accessories of gold, silver, and copper remained. These were similar to the accoutrements portrayed on the statue in the dining hall. A decorative buckle, all that remained of a belt, bore the same water dragon crest. Was this the man who'd inspired the statue? If not, then a descendant, perhaps?

A discolored, human-shaped outline surrounded the skeleton, indicating the man had still had flesh when laid to rest here. Or had he lain down here himself? How had he reached his end? There was no way of knowing.

I saw no sign that the intact treasures he wore had been tampered with. The sage evidently had cared only for his research, not for riches. Or else, he'd had too much respect to desecrate this man's corpse. That was the feeling I got, anyway. This body was meant to remain here undisturbed, the man kept at eternal rest. Almost all of this man's world had fallen to pieces along with him. Shouldn't I feel responsible for preserving those remains?

I shook off these heavy thoughts and looked around me, quickly spotting a small writing desk in a corner. It was wood, and not particularly old. Clearly, the sage had brought it himself, but how had he transported it? I could only imagine he'd taken it apart and reassembled it here. The thought of that man desperately dragging scraps of wood through that narrow corridor without being seen was somewhat amusing. He'd devoted himself to his research here, with no one—not even a sound—to disturb him. I could easily picture him bent over his desk in silence, with the skeleton as his only company. This image fit the old man perfectly.

I gently pulled open the desk's drawer, finding nothing inside but a pen and dried inkwell. According to the sage, the documents were hidden in a secret compartment, a hiding spot within this hiding spot. How exciting. It was all enough to quicken a young child's heart.

As instructed, I pressed my leg against the desk's leg, grabbed the desktop, and slid it sideways. I then pulled it up and opened the drawer halfway. I lifted the desktop higher until it clicked and came completely free.

After placing the top to one side, I looked inside the desk to find a space that ran deeper than the drawer. Resting in this space was what I had come here for: a hefty book. Its cover was identical to that of the temple's scriptures, but its contents were not. Certainly this had helped the old man disguise his work, but I thought it was also an expression of his defiant spirit.

I opened the book and flipped through it. Next to the written characters used by humanity in this world, which I had grown accustomed to seeing, were lines of bizarre text I had never seen before. This was the grand culmination of the sage's research. A lexicon of orcish, camouflaged as scripture.

After retrieving the dictionary, I inserted my hand into the mouth of the face in the crypt and was transported back to the room beyond the dining hall. Having retraced my path through the tunnel, I sneaked out of the hole behind the statue, taking great care not to be seen. However, as I stepped out of the statue's shadow, my eyes met with those of a priest eating at one of the tables. He was startled by my sudden appearance, but after shaking his weary head, returned to his meal.

I left the dining hall and entered the main chamber, where over a thousand priests mumbled their spells and injected their mana. It felt so noisy after spending time in that forgotten crypt.

However, it was simultaneously comforting to be surrounded by the living. I had made it back from the world beyond, I myself, alive.

Carrying the faux scriptures under my arm, an innocent look on my face, I started crossing the chamber only to run into Worion, who was apparently making his rounds.

"Oh, Hero! I see you're back already."

"Yes, I was blessed with good winds. I'm sorry I haven't dropped by to see you."

Worion glanced at the tome I carried.

"How was it there? Did you find your writing teacher?"

"Yes, he's quite the character. He transcribed these sacred texts and told me to use them to study the correct words and syntax and such."

"I see. Very good...but that volume looks especially valuable. Take care not to lose it."

I had the suspicion he already knew what was in the book.

"Of course. My teacher told me to bring it back without a scratch."

"Incidentally, do you have paper already? You'll need a lot for writing practice."

"I was just about to arrange for some."

"In that case, I'll get you some of our stock. We should be able to spare a bundle for our hero."

Worion called over one of the younger priests. Then, after assuring me the ceremony continued to go smoothly, he resumed making his rounds.

The boy priest told me, "I'll show you to the storehouse. This way."

It wasn't long before I returned to the house where George awaited me, bearing a heavy bundle of paper.

"Welcome back, Hero," George greeted me from the doorway. "Umm, what's that?"

"We can talk later. Clear some space."

The floor of the house was bare dirt. I had my reservations about placing valuable parchment directly upon it.

"Of course. Give me a moment."

George called over the old housekeeper, and together they swiftly cleared the table of its plates and utensils.

With a little "heave-ho," I deposited the paper and disguised book there. And now to...do what? Concerned for the book's safety, I wanted to send it to the manor in Kadann Hill immediately, to be placed under heavy protection. Torson was trustworthy enough to handle that. However, I also wanted to make use of it first. On top of that, if it was possible, I wanted to have the contents copied so I would have a version for myself.

I reminded myself that I had permission to copy it, but I needed to take extra precautions to make sure it never reached the eyes of anyone who couldn't be trusted.

"I don't care if you copy my work," the sage had told me, "but don't trust another to do that, and don't give your copy to a bookbinder. For the binding, I'll introduce you to someone once I arrive there. This person's blind, so he can bind any book without knowing its contents, as long as the pages are already ordered. Don't reveal the book to anyone else! I know how idiots like you can barely control yourselves."

I told the housekeeper to go take a break at the bar. After confirming the old lady had left with her coin purse, I called George over.

"George, can you keep a secret?"

"Yes, of course." He gave me an odd look.

"Leaking this secret could prove fatal, so are you certain?"

"I swear to God I can. My life already belongs to you."

"Even if it goes against God's teachings?" I pressed.

That question took him by surprise. He seemed to process the import of my words, but he finally stood more upright, and firmly stated, "Yes, Hero."

"Very good. Then I have one request. I want you to copy the contents of this book here. Have you ever done that before?" I asked, gingerly stroking the pages.

"Yes, copying the scriptures was part of my priestly training."

His quizzical expression seemed to ask, *What part of that goes against God's teachings?*

"Open it."

I gestured toward the book on the table, and he opened its cover.

"Hero... I've never seen these letters. What are they?"

"You don't need to know. All I can say is, it has to do with my work. In any case, I want you to copy all of it."

"Understood."

George wasn't a fool. He likely had a vague idea of what this was. After all, he had closely witnessed my attempts to teach Johnny.

"Before you get to work, I need you to swear again that you'll keep this a secret."

I didn't know how effective a vow would be to him, but it was better than nothing.

"Yes, I swear it not only to God, but on the name of my father. I will protect this secret."

From what I'd heard from Thret, that man had been adored by his children, so I didn't take George's vow lightly.

During our exchange, Johnny shambled over. She noticed the open book on the table, gazed at its pages, and began jumping for joy. Early on, she—and I had to remind myself she *was* a she—had been so timid, but she had grown much more relaxed of late, so I could tell George had been quite welcoming to her.

George glanced at me to gauge my reaction. I gave him a nod, and he lifted Johnny higher so she could get a better look at the book.

To proceed, I was going to have to find an orc who could read. It would be so much easier if Johnny could read, but I didn't have high hopes of that. What were the literacy rates of orcs, anyway? The orcs mostly fought with muskets—muzzle-loader guns. If their cultural development paralleled the advancements of my world, their literacy rates would still be relatively low. Additionally, the ones the humans captured were all farmers and soldiers, so it was unlikely she had received sufficient education.

I didn't want to give in to pessimism about finding a literate orc. Surely their army's high-ranking officers would be literate. And in any humble village, human or orcish, there always had to be one or two people who could read. There had to be an orc in captivity I could make use of... If only I knew—

Johnny was feverishly oinking at the book's contents. She twisted her way out of George's grasp, stole the ash-covered poker from beside the woodburning stove, and began scratching something into the dirt floor.

What? Could it be...?

I snatched up the book, searching for any symbols that resembled the ones Johnny had written. I flipped through page after page. The dictionary was ordered by human words, which had been written first, with the corresponding orc words gradually filled in later.

I scanned the entire book front to back before I was able to find the three symbols Johnny had written.

"I"

"Read"

"Words"

We'd already hit the jackpot.

Nearly two months had gone by since I'd acquired the orcish dictionary. The barrier ceremony had continued smoothly, and I would soon be freed from my monotonous position. Meanwhile, my lessons with Johnny proceeded at a rapid pace. Through learning their language, I was also gaining a bit of understanding about orcish society.

I had asked to Johnny write her true name. When I compared the words she'd written to the dictionary, I found hers corresponded to the human words for "white" and "flower." A sweet, girly name. The letters she used were somewhat different from those in the book, but perhaps they were modified when used for proper names. I would need to ask the sage about that.

Nevertheless, I needed to change her name accordingly. I wasn't someone who would arbitrarily come up with a demeaning name like "Potato." However, it being impossible for me to match orcish pronunciation, I decided to go for something similar to what I'd decoded.

"Listen up. Your name is Lily. I'm going to call you Lily now."

She just stared at me blankly. I pointed at her again and again, repeating, "Lily, Lily," until finally she seemed to catch on. Thereafter, she responded to her new, more suitable name.

For one exercise, I flipped through the dictionary while asking her if there was anything in its pages she would like to have. She had progressed from writing on the dirt floor to writing on paper, so in small letters she meekly inked the word "clothes." It was winter, after all, and quite cold, but I wondered if maybe it was also a matter of modesty, since she lived among clothed humans. I promptly asked the housekeeper to see about making her some clothing that would fit her orcish frame, and then continued with my questions.

From what I gleaned through piecing together her writing, she'd been the personal maid of a certain orcish noble. Unfortunately, while out patrolling their territory a few years prior, the noble she served along with her and the rest of the servants had been the victims of an out-of-season human attack, and they had all been captured. Those who'd attacked them had been dressed in white, undoubtedly the Knights Templar led by Princess Liana. Lily and her companions were soon taken to a slave market. She didn't know the fate of the rest, but she herself was sold to the grain mill, where she had ultimately met me.

Beyond her personal history, I started to gain a bigger picture as well, and I soon feared humanity's situation was more dire than I had imagined. The opponent we contended with was a single provincial lord of a massive orc empire made up of smaller states. The main state of this union possessed over three times the number of soldiers as the lord's personal force, and with all their provinces taken together, that number would be increased tenfold.

Not to mention, there were numerous other orc countries outside of this empire.

With these facts before me, saving humanity by eliminating the orcs seemed but a naïve dream. The orcs saw the humans as troublesome beasts that had descended the mountains into their territory in the fall. They were left to roam free simply because it would be too much trouble to cross the mountains to hunt them all down.

Up to that point, I'd held to a vague idea of seizing victory in one great battle and using that victory as leverage for peaceful negotiations. In light of this information, it seemed that would prove difficult. Still, if we could defeat that one provincial lord, that would make the rest of the orcs take us seriously.

Meanwhile, I needed to somehow keep the humans in check, lest they stir up the hive too much, but how was I supposed to contain them when they headed out for their incursions come next fall? In the first place, their finances depended in no small part on plunder. It might've been a mistake to disperse the blockade with air raids. If the valley had remained sealed, it would have been impossible to send any more armies through. If we stopped this plundering, perhaps then the orcs would take a less hostile view toward us.

No, we couldn't depend on them growing benevolent. They had tried to destroy Dragonjaw Gate with their massive cannons. If we didn't use force against them preemptively, they would try to destroy the wall again. So what was I supposed to do? I was losing confidence in my ability to save this world.

PLANET OF THE ORCS

CHAPTER 7

NIGHT RAID

THE BLACK DOG watched his men and their aquilups struggle to cross the precarious cliffs of Dragonbone Ridge. It would have been impossible on foot, but the aquilups were native to the mountains and could span the distance. Not completely unharmed, however, as the mountains were especially dangerous at night. Even as he looked on, one of the aquilups slipped, and down it plummeted with its rider still on its back. The Black Dog's heart lurched. He knew the man's name, knew everything about him, from his early life to his family structure. Had he died on the battlefield, the Black Dog could have accepted the loss, but it being an accidental death, on a mission where the Black Dog had dragged him along, it pierced him like a dagger.

The Black Dog withdrew a large blue gemstone and stared at it, rolling it around in his palm as he recalled the day of the festival.

That day, the Black Dog had been summoned to the margrave's bedroom. The old orc lay on a large bed, surrounded by many statesmen, and he muttered in delirium.

"Daughter... My daughter..."

His eyes were all but lifeless. The rumors were true, then, that he was knocking on death's door. One of his closest aides bent to whisper in his ear, informing him of the Black Dog's arrival.

A touch of light returned to the margrave's eyes. A tenacious light that defied the grasp of death, tinged with a kind of madness.

"O-oh...good... You're here. Come closer."

The statesmen cleared a path to the bed. Seeing the Black Dog standing there, the margrave spoke with feeble breath.

"I have...a request. My daughter... Reclaim my daughter."

He really had lost his mind. His daughter, his second child, had been missing for three years now. This was the same daughter who had offered the Black Dog her hand in marriage. She was a lively woman who cared for her territory, and that had been her downfall. While surveying land near the human domain, she had encountered an off-season band of raiders and been taken captive. Not a single orc had ever returned from beyond the mountains. Rumors abounded as to what had happened to the kidnapped orcs, but there was no way to learn of their fates for sure. For all intents and purposes, his daughter was considered dead. The margrave had doted on his bright and cheerful girl, and therefore fell into a great despair, his health sharply declining ever since.

The Black Dog came closer, his snorts heavy and grim.

"Leave it to me. I will bring her back, no matter what."

Hearing this, the margrave gave a satisfied smile and slowly closed his eyes. The statesmen stirred nervously, assuming the worst, but his steady breathing reassured them, and the doctor in attendance ushered them out of the room.

As he and the others were leaving, the Black Dog ran into the person he had least expected to see—the margrave's failure of a son. The son, and a number of his followers, urged the Black Dog into the margrave's study. After taking a seat at the margrave's desk, the lazy son grinned at him repugnantly, his curling tusks gleaming.

"You made an oath in there. You swore to my dying father that you would reclaim my sister. You swore before everyone."

His words received stern nods from his entourage. "We definitely heard the man make an oath."

The Black Dog grimaced. What was he supposed to say?

"There's nothing more serious than an oath made to a man on his deathbed. So, do you have a plan?"

Still the Black Dog did not speak.

The son sneered, and from a pocket he produced a round object. "I thought not. In that case, I have something for you. Take it."

It was a blue gemstone, about the size of an orc fist.

"Our researchers found it in the ruins. Supposedly, it has the power to destroy that irksome wall."

The Black Dog accepted the stone. He saw it had a uniform transparency, but complex and minute three-dimensional symbols were spread throughout its interior. It was beautiful, no doubt, but he found it hard to believe something like this could bring down the humans' wall.

"I see you don't believe me, but look at this."

The son waved his hand to one of his cronies. The statesman produced a report and passed it to the Black Dog, who flipped it open. What he saw took him by surprise.

It was a rough blueprint of the fortress. At the very least, it matched what he had seen of the fortress from standing beneath it. Yet the diagrams didn't end with its outer appearance. The report also covered its interior in great detail. The drawings were all too precise to only be an artist's speculations.

The son looked pleased with the Black Dog's astonishment.

"The researchers found these documents along with the stone. How about it, then? Does it look useful?"

While the Black Dog hated to admit it, the son was right. It did look useful, if it was accurate.

"And they found more than just blueprints. There's a description in there of how to use the stone as well. You've seen magic for yourself, haven't you?"

The orcs knew about the magic the humans used, but they'd never taken it too seriously. Mostly they saw it as folk incantations the savages used in the hope of protection from orc bullets. Until recently, when he'd witnessed it for himself, the Black Dog hadn't believed in it much either.

"From what we understand, if the gemstone is applied to a certain critical point, it will counteract the human magic. Their spell will be broken, and the wall itself will crumble."

He couldn't write this off as only a tall tale. It was possible that whoever had built the fortress had prepared measures in case it ever fell into enemy hands. Word had it that what the orcs called the

Ghost City had once been the capital of an ancient human civilization. Could the Black Dog really believe in the jewel's authenticity?

"As the proxy margrave of the northern territory, I order you to lead your barbarians to the wall, and ascertain the truth of the matter."

If the margrave himself had ordered him, perhaps the Black Dog would have seen it as a stirring adventure, but this untrustworthy son only stoked his resentment.

With a vulgar smile on his face, the lazy son snorted. "I don't expect you to do it for free. If you manage to destroy the wall, it will become possible to invade the territory of the hairless apes, and then perhaps you really will be able to reclaim my sister. If you see this mission through, then regardless of whether the stone is effective, I will acknowledge that you fulfilled your oath and put in your best effort. Then you will be free. If the wall does collapse, I'll even appoint you as the official commander of our expeditionary forces. Of course, if you dislike the idea of working under me, I'll write you a favorable letter of recommendation to work elsewhere. You should be able to become guard captain of any city you choose. So what do you think? Not a bad deal, right?"

When the Black Dog did not answer, he pressed further.

"If you turn down this order and flee, I'll put up wanted posters throughout the empire, saying you deserted before the enemy. Oh, you could air your grievances about that, but between a decree with the northern margrave's seal and the arguments of a lowly mercenary barbarian, which side would people believe?"

What recourse did the Black Dog have?

"Remember, this is a top-secret mission. Don't tell a soul. We can wait until your wounds have healed to put it in motion. Just do your best putting together a plan that doesn't get you killed, okay?" His laughter filled the room.

Even while the Black Dog was lost in this memory, his aquilup partner, who had accompanied him for many long years, pressed on without missing a step. Meanwhile, a messenger came rushing toward him from the front of the expedition, bearing an important report from their scouts. Having heard the report, the Black Dog shook free of his bitter thoughts, focusing on the here and now. He raced his aquilup to rendezvous with the scouts.

The scouts looked down over the valley, having concealed themselves among the summit's rocks. Upon noticing the Black Dog's approach, one of them readied a space for him. The Black Dog edged into the gap, carefully taking a peek below at the great wall with a massive lake behind it. This was the first time he had seen the wall from this angle. In fact, this might have been the first time any orc had. He took out the documents the son had given him and compared them with his view. The layout matched to an uncanny degree.

It was as if this confirmed to him that the mission was not nonsense. The Black Dog felt a chill run down his spine, and he unconsciously rubbed his flank. The wound there had already healed, and he had ordered a new breastplate be made. The armor-smith had proudly told him, "I put a little something in there to protect you," but he didn't know if it would actually prove useful.

Calling a few veterans over, he quickly set to work laying out their next moves. Now all he could do was pray that the fortress continued to match the blueprints.

I was having a nightmare, a different one from usual. I dreamed of what would have happened if I'd been allowed to stay in my first world. It was a peaceful world with no war, where I lived with that girl. We were happy as could be, and I had no complaints. And yet, I still didn't feel alive. While the girl smiled beside me so contentedly, I was ever tormented with the feeling that something was missing. My directionless impulses swelled as a black whirlwind within me, slowly eating away at my mind.

Until finally—

I woke up. Such a horribly realistic dream. My heart went on pounding madly. I couldn't remember what my dream-self had planned to do. Or maybe I didn't want to remember.

I had propped my sword against the bed, and I reached now to pull it close. The heavy weight of steel helped me regain a bit of calm. The metal fittings of its hilt were soothingly cool to the touch. Still, a strange unease lingered. For a moment, I puzzled over it. Then I realized this unease I felt was the familiar intuition that danger was imminent. War was close, the enemy near. This wasn't some dream.

I leapt out of bed, changed in a hurry, and equipped my sword.

I hadn't brought any armor here with me, as it was better to fly light, the most I had being leather gauntlets and greaves. I rushed out of the main tower, but it was silent outside, with not a ripple on the surface of the water as it reflected the twinkling stars. Flames were lit here and there, where soldiers were on watch.

A cold wind blew, making the flames waver. So far, there was no sign of anything awry, but I was convinced something was about to happen. I went to seek out Herbert, captain of the garrison, who was surely in his room at this hour. I didn't want to wake him, but I needed him to increase security.

However, when I started back to the central tower, I heard an alarm raised from elsewhere. I turned toward the voice to see a lookout pointing and crying out. I raced up to the parapet and peered into the valley below. Countless flickering lights dotted the darkness, and there was no way they were carried by human hands. They were orcs.

How had they gotten this close without being spotted? Despite the dragon patrols, there hadn't been any reports of an advancing orc force. They had to have hidden during the day and moved only at nighttime, when dragons had more trouble flying.

The watchtower's alarm bells rang piercingly. Silent only moments ago, the fortress had now burst into activity. Soldiers poured out of the central tower, racing toward their stations.

It was not long before Herbert appeared beside me with his guards.

"This isn't good. How is the barrier?" he asked.

"Today, Worion reported it would take another week."

The magic circle had already begun to emit a pale light, but it had yet to reach the point of activation. That being said, it was progressing more quickly than expected.

Herbert groaned in frustration, but said, "We should be able to repel them, so long as they don't have cannons." He leaned out from a crenel in the parapet and tried to pierce the darkness with his eyes.

"Be careful!" His guards lunged to pull him back, but Herbert didn't budge.

"Don't get in the way! They're out of firing range!"

He was right in that the constellation of torches was still a good distance from the wall, but because of this distance, I couldn't make out who exactly we were up against.

Herbert drew back and asked one of his men, "Did you send a messenger to town?"

"Yes, sir! More men are being awakened and readied."

"And to the dragon house?"

"Also done. A message should reach the capital by sunrise."

It was a new moon that night. I felt sorry for the rider who would have to fly through the utter darkness.

"Good. Now go to the priests underground. Get us some war priests."

"Yes, sir!"

The guard rushed off to relay this order.

"What about me, Herbert?" I asked.

He looked a bit troubled. "Hero... I leave that to your discretion. You may help in whatever capacity you deem best."

Being that I was field marshal, he probably didn't feel comfortable issuing me orders, which was fine by me. I was grateful for the freedom to move and act as I wished.

First, I needed to gauge the enemy's movements. I looked into the valley again. Something was bothering me. They had come so far without being noticed—why light their torches now?

I considered a few possibilities.

One: They had lit the torches to regroup their formation, which had drifted apart on their march through the darkness. They had determined there would be more casualties if they attacked without proper organization. This made a surprise attack impossible, but at least they hadn't been detected earlier, and we were still scrambling to meet their attack.

Two: They were assembling or preparing something and needed the light. Perhaps they were readying cannons, or just setting up camps that could endure the water this time. If they had brought in materials during the day, they would have been washed away before construction could begin. However, the footing of the valley had only gotten worse since it was last flooded. Could they really work under those conditions?

They were both dangerous gambles. It would be all over for them if we simply opened the floodgates. Unless our opening the gates was their objective. Did they actually hope we'd panic and empty the dam, so a larger force could move through behind them? I felt this third possibility was quite feasible.

On to the fourth: The lights were a distraction to draw our

attention. Since they were so conspicuous, they might be nothing but misdirection. If so, what was their real point of attack?

Dragonjaw Gate was protected on both sides by steep mountains, and it was winter, no less. Even if it didn't snow very much around here, sending soldiers through those cold mountains in the dead of the night would be—

"Beak-dogs!" Herbert suddenly shouted. He'd arrived at the thought before me. "Those monsters would be able to race along the slopes! These lights are just a decoy! Their true aim is the gate tower! They plan on infiltrating the gate and opening it for their army! We can hold them off so long as we protect the gate!"

He ordered his men, "Gather soldiers in the east! Increase security around the sluice gate's controls!"

After sending all his guards off, Herbert sprinted for the gate tower himself. Herbert seemed to have made the right call, but my own doubts remained. Was that really all there was to it? A formless intuition continued to prod me. I peered into the valley again, but aside from the torches, I couldn't make out the enemy no matter how I strained my eyes.

Soon, a number of warpriests raced out of the small western watchtower. It was clear they had raced up all those stairs from the underground chamber at full speed, and I pitied them for it. Would they be able to perform their services in such a breathless state?

The sound of gunshots carried to me from the east side of the fortress. There followed screams, the groans of injured soldiers, and the horrible roars of beasts. Combat had begun, undoubtedly a beak-dog attack. So had Herbert been correct?

I saw the faces of the winded warpriests tense up at the sounds. Below me, they kneeled and began preparing a magic circle. One of them handed a prepared talisman to a soldier, who raced off toward the gate tower. Meanwhile, guards surrounded the priests in a close-knit formation, protective talismans already affixed to their shields.

I leaned out from the parapet again, watching the valley. Those flickering torches showed no change in their position, even though combat had begun. There was no doubt about it now—some major strategic plan was underway. This was different from the skirmishes and burnings. This was real war, and it set my blood astir. As inappropriate as it might've seemed, I couldn't restrain the smile that came to my face.

No more holding back. This was a genuine battle for the future of humanity, and I would relish it all I cared to. So I raced off in search of the inevitable commander, who had to be somewhere close.

In front of the gate tower, the soldiers under Herbert's command fought tooth and nail.

Beak-dogs would leap from the darkness, the orcs on their backs raining down bullets from the handguns they carried. Guards would drop with each volley, but the line didn't falter. A row of spears prevented the beak-dogs from breaching the line, and crossbow bolts would fly at the backs of the orcs as they retreated to reload.

The garrison at Dragonjaw Gate was different from the ruffians, mercenaries, and farmer conscripts the lords made use of. These were soldiers by trade who trained day in and day out, the majority of them experienced veterans.

Dragonjaw Gate's walls were impressively wide. Even the narrowest part of the wall was at least thirty paces across. Where the gate tower met the highway was a plaza over two hundred paces from end to end. This was where Herbert had deployed his troops in a fan, defending the entrance to the fortress. When the attack had first begun, the soldiers who'd hurried there could only form a thin line. However, reinforcements continued to arrive from all over the fort, and now the wall of fighters was more densely filled out.

Almost had us there, Herbert thought with a chuckle. Had he been late in making the call, perhaps the enemy would have overrun the gate tower. He had been away from the battlefield for quite some time, but he was happy to know his instincts hadn't grown dull just yet.

A little later than he had hoped, talismans charged by the warpriests started to arrive. Herbert had the soldiers at the forefront affix these to their shields during gaps between attacks, and in the blink of an eye, the talismans' protective magic came into effect.

The orcs fired a volley of bullets, which simply bounced off the barrier with pale blue sparks. Seeing this, Herbert was already convinced of their victory.

"Push the line forward!"

On his command, the crossbowmen in the back unleashed their bolts at once to support the vanguard as it charged in an unbroken line. The beak-dogs that had encroached on the open plaza fled back to the slopes in a panic, disappearing into the mountains.

Shame, shame! Herbert thought. *Always so quick to run!*

His soldiers advanced to the foot of the mountains, finishing off straggler orcs who had failed to escape in time. Here, they stopped. Herbert was irritated that he had failed to do any real damage to the enemy force, but he was satisfied that he'd managed to drive them back. However, no sooner had these orcs fled than others began firing from the forest.

They fired from various locations, yet all their shots were concentrated on a single point: the vanguard. The barrier was broken, a number of soldiers dropping to writhe in pain. Herbert both cursed and admired the orcs' marksmanship.

How can this be?! How do they fire like that in the dark? What now?

Chasing them into the mountains would be like running into a trap. However, it was clear that remaining here would only increase their casualties. In the corner of his eye, Herbert noticed something that was reflecting moonlight. The others might not have noticed yet, but Herbert was a warrior who had survived many a battlefield. This something was coming from the village. Reinforcements! The soldiers who'd gone into the village for some rest were coming back.

These reinforcements were headed right toward them despite having no torches by which to spot them. No doubt the returning soldiers had cleverly determined their position by triangulating the streams of enemy gunfire.

This turn of events inspired Herbert's next move.

"Pull back! Retreat to the gate!"

First, he would need to draw the beak-dogs back into the plaza. They would exchange fire to hold them there until the village reinforcements could flank them. Depending on the timing, the new force might even be able to surround the beak-dog riders. The reinforcements were not a significant force, but what they lacked in numbers they could make up for with a sneak attack. Herbert sent a runner to meet the reinforcements, all the while slowly pulling his line back. He simply needed to wait for the enemy to answer this invitation.

As expected, the riders appeared in the open space once more. In unison, the crossbowmen launched their bolts, but this hardly damaged the prowling beak-dogs. Whenever the orcs fired, however, one or two of Herbert's fighters would fall.

Just you wait!

Suddenly, there was another flash of concentrated fire from out of the darkness, off to one side. Herbert heard one of his men scream along with vicious, bestial roars.

So there was a separate unit of beak-dogs as well. The reinforcements had fallen victim to a surprise attack themselves. Herbert gritted his teeth in frustration. His plan had been thwarted, but he still maintained his composure.

They haven't landed a decisive blow either. As long as they don't capture the gate tower, they will never see victory. Morning will come, the dragons will fly, and we will win. Their handguns cannot take down dragons.

That was when he heard gunshots behind him.

Behind? The majority of his forces had gathered at the gate, which lay to the east. Only a minimum number of troops remained to the west.

"Form a half-circle around the gate!" Herbert shouted. To a messenger, he ordered, "Tell the warpriests to get back underground!"

The messenger sprinted away to pass the order on to the warpriests, who were chanting their protection magic.

We should be able to hold here, even if the enemy comes with twice the numbers, and we have guards at the sluice gate controls. But... Herbert had his doubts about the western tower, which had been left all but defenseless. If the enemy got inside and infiltrated the underground chamber, that would put both the magic circle and the priests working on it in great danger.

No, the orcs couldn't possibly know about the circle, he thought, shaking off that ominous notion. Their current distribution should suffice. He couldn't afford to disperse the troops any further. And yet, the enemies he heard firing in the west never appeared here at the gate tower.

Don't tell me they really did...

His face went pale.

The Black Dog raced his aquilup partner toward the western edge of Dragonjaw Gate. Five riders accompanied him, all of them elites among elites, the last surviving friends from the earliest days of his career. Together they charged headlong up the slopes and then leapt through the air onto the wall.

Taken by surprise, the lookout here was cut down before he could shout. Three others realized what was happening and readied their spears to meet the Black Dog's advance, but his men fired their guns, bringing them down.

He spotted another human running off to spread news of the attack. While a good amount of distance separated them, the Black Dog got a bullet in the human with little effort. There was no time to reload, though, so he dropped the spent handgun into a side pouch and produced another one from his belt.

So far, things were going as planned. The enemy had gathered their forces at the gate on the eastern edge of the fortress, leaving only a few lookouts on this side. However, that wouldn't last long. These gunshots would alert the humans.

He made quick work of the lookouts at the entrance of the western tower and rushed into it without dismounting. His agile aquilup raced up the narrow spiral staircase.

They were at the top of the tower in no time. A soldier there thrust a spear at him, but the aquilup smoothly dodged it, then went for his throat. That was all it took. Having jumped down from the saddle, the Black Dog consulted the blueprints the margrave's son had given him. He searched for the statue marked therein, and located it soon enough. When he lifted it away, a section of the floor opened without a sound, revealing a separate stairway down. So far, everything corresponded with the diagrams. He was almost surprised at himself for the excitement he felt.

Unfortunately, the aquilups couldn't fit into this stairwell. He and his men were forced to descend the narrow passage on foot, moving as quickly as they could down the tall steps that had been designed for human feet.

When finally reached the bottom of the staircase, the sight before him left the Black Dog at a loss for words. It was a vast space, the entirety of the floor covered by symbols that gave off a pale blue light. Faint, luminous traces of mana floated up from them here and there, like bubbles in a breeze.

In the center of all this stood a single human.

The human's lips spread the moment he recognized them. Reflecting the eerie light at his feet, the human's eyes glowed fiercely. His appearance was uncanny yet almost divine. The Black Dog was frozen in place and remained unmoving even when the human's right hand flashed.

All of a sudden, the Black Dog's vision lurched as someone thrust him out of the way. A trail of light whizzed through the spot where he had just been standing. The rider who'd saved him had taken the spear of light in his place and crumpled to the ground.

The Black Dog snapped back to his senses. He lifted his gun and pulled the trigger, his four remaining comrades doing the same. The human instantly manifested a shield and blocked every bullet. At the same time, he charged at them.

The Black Dog ducked to avoid the sweep of another spear of light, drew his saber, and slashed with it. Before the blade could touch him, the human lashed out one of his long legs in a side kick that struck the Black Dog in the stomach. Blown off his feet by the powerful kick, the orc smacked into the wall.

The air had left his lungs, and he choked in agony, his body too stunned to move. The thick metal armor covering his abdomen had actually been dented. He wanted to laugh incredulously at this, but only a rasping breath escaped his lips.

Two of his longtime war buddies launched a perfectly coordinated attack from both sides, but the monster in human form dodged them and severed their swords with a spear of light gripped in each hand. Without missing a beat, the Black Dog's friends threw down the hilts of their broken swords and lunged forward to grab at the human with their hands. Meanwhile, the other two used this opportunity to attack the human from behind.

Yet the human avoided even this move without difficulty, practically gliding along the ground as he stabbed his spear into one rider after another. It took only a few seconds, and the Black Dog could only watch in horror.

This man was as strong as a demon. No, not even that. A demon king.

I see—he is *the Demon King!* But the Black Dog didn't have time to wonder why he was here. Of course the Demon King would be here! Why wouldn't he be? He cursed his own ignorance for failing to predict this outcome.

By the time he was back on his feet his friends were all dead, but he wouldn't run away with his tail between his legs. No matter the outcome, he must try to avenge his comrades.

He held his saber at the ready. The motion made the Demon King's lips pull even wider, baring his small human canines. He extinguished his light spears and drew his own sword from its scabbard.

The Black Dog was relieved to see this. His legs were still quivering, and he knew he wouldn't be able to dodge a spear throw. If he could only dive past his foe's blade, there was a slight chance he might land a deadly strike.

As they circled each other, he slowly and cautiously closed the distance between them. Suddenly, an odd chill ran down his spine, and he stopped advancing. By some intuition he *knew* he couldn't risk a single step closer. The human was beyond his reach as well. The gap between them seemed to hang there, waiting for one of them to misstep and close it.

Nervousness had made his breathing uneven. The Demon King stepped forward ever so slightly. The Black Dog could feel the coil of death tighten around his body.

The next instant, the Demon King pounced. With a sweep of his sword, he easily knocked the Black Dog's saber right out of his grip. The orc's center of balance was thrown off by the impact, which left his front open to another kick. He hit the floor, rolling, and when he came to a rest, the Demon King planted a foot on his chest. The monster held the tip of his sword blade to the Black Dog's throat. The orc couldn't read human expressions, but he had no doubt the Demon King felt triumphant. Still, he just kept the point of his sword there without thrusting, their intense gazes locked.

Fool! I was waiting for this! The Black Dog's sword hand was numb from having the blade knocked out of it, but he still managed to tug—with all his might—on a thin thread that had gone unnoticed.

There was a sharp bang. The gun incorporated into his breastplate fired a deadly shot.

When I saw all the surprise attacks play out without any change to the torches in the valley, I was sure of it—the raids were just a distraction. If the enemy really wanted to break through the gate, there was no way the army in the valley wouldn't have budged. Even if the present force had managed to take control of the gate, if that were truly the plan, there was no telling if they would be able to hold it without those supposed reinforcements. No, that torch-bearing army would have to be close by and ready to immediately lend support. Their real objective lay elsewhere.

The surprise attacks were drawing nearly all our troops to the east. It stood to reason their true target lay to the west, but what would they want there? It could only be the entrance to the underground chamber. At the moment, the majority of the temple's priests who could use mana were gathered there. If the enemy got to them, the priests would be massacred. Protection magic was the greatest defense humanity had against the orcish armies. Losing the priests would shatter humanity's hope for resistance.

There were other possibilities. Perhaps the enemies on the west side hoped to get over the wall to attack the garrison from within. Or maybe they intended to take the central tower and render the floodgates useless. It was possible the orcs didn't know about the gathered priests, and how could they ever know about the hidden entrance to the underground chamber?

Yet my gut firmly told me the underground chamber had to be their goal.

I didn't often rely on my instincts, but on the off chance the enemy made it there, it truly would be a national crisis. I needed to stop it no matter what it took. If I was wrong, then so be it. I could just help out whoever needed me after that. I'd at least check, and if I was wrong I'd lend my strength elsewhere.

I raced for the western tower, plunged inside, and pounded up the stairs. I ordered the lookout I encountered there to let me know if any enemies should appear. Then, I opened the entrance to the secret passage and raced down the long stairwell to the underground chamber.

There were two reasons I didn't wait to watch for enemies atop the wall. Firstly, if they came in great numbers, there was a chance those beak-dogs of theirs would just jump over me anyway and slip past. Secondly, if they did try to infiltrate the underground chamber, I could bottleneck them in the narrow stairway and hold them off until Herbert sent help. Additionally, the stairwell would hamper the use of their beak-dogs, so I probably didn't have to worry about them.

Rushing into the chamber, I immediately called out for Worion and told him to evacuate all the priests into the surrounding rooms. They had nowhere to run if I failed, but it was too late to lead them out through the tower. Still, I was feeling pretty good about my odds.

Soon enough, my instincts proved correct, and orcs appeared in the chamber. They didn't immediately attack, though. I didn't know how many of them would come, so I told myself I mustn't wait for more than ten to arrive before I acted.

One, two, three... Soon there were six, but no more. I actually felt a little disappointed, but I recognized a familiar face among them, and a satisfied smile came to my lips.

The one-eyed orc...the one who'd dodged my spear thrust from behind during our first retreat. The Black Dog, was it? I'd asked around and found he was well known among the humans too.

If he was leading them, his companions could be no regular orcs, but select elites—worthy adversaries. Yet for some reason, none of the orcs moved. Then again, I couldn't blame them. With no priests to obscure the glowing symbols that covered the floor, the sight of it was eerie and unsettling. It looked like the orcs needed a wake-up call.

I manifested a spear and hurled it at the Black Dog. However, the large orc beside him reacted before his master could. He pushed the dazzled Black Dog out of the way and took my spear of light to the lungs.

That was enough to wake them up. They pulled the guns holstered at their hips and began firing, but I quickly formed a shield and repelled the bullets. Before they could change their tactic, I charged at the Black Dog. I swept at the orcs with my spear, and they all managed to dodge it, just barely. That was how it had to be.

I didn't want to kill the Black Dog just yet. I needed to demand he tell me how he'd known to come here. I evaded his saber and kicked him in the midsection with all my might. He slammed into the wall by the entrance, then slumped to the floor.

Before I could take a breath, an orc flew in on either side of me. If possible, I wanted them all alive, in case one proved more talkative than the others, so I formed a spear in both hands and merely severed their blades. However, they dropped their broken swords and attempted to seize hold of me with their hands. This was getting too dangerous. While orcs were small, they could overpower in numbers, so I nimbly jumped to avoid them.

The remaining two orcs came at me from behind, hoping to catch me by surprise. *Dammit! When did one of them get behind me?!* They'd even attacked with a calculated delay just long enough that it would make it hard to dodge.

I dematerialized one of my spears so I could reach out for the nearer of the two fighters, grabbing the hand that held his saber and pulling him in close. Shock showed in his face as I used his momentum to spin him through the air. With that spin, I avoided the lunge of the second of the two behind me.

From the corner of my eye, I could see the Black Dog preparing to drag himself back to his feet, and I decided to give up on taking the others alive.

First, I hammered my spear of light into the one who was currently charging me. I leapt back to dodge a second one, simultaneously skewering an orc who was going for my flank with a saber. As I whirled around, I swept the legs out from under another saber-wielder. It was then that the one I'd just dodged managed to grab on to my leg. The surviving saber orc stood up and made to thrust at me, but he was too late. By that time, I'd already stabbed the orc clinging to my leg, kicked off his body, and jumped sideways.

The last orc whipped his head wildly, as if he'd lost sight of me. What he found was a spear through his torso.

Oh, they'd been formidable. There weren't many who could fight me to that extent, even among the humans. Yet they were now gone, and I turned my eyes back to the Black Dog. To my surprise, he was already on his feet. His legs were visibly shaking, but he was upright, and I almost admired him for that.

Even more surprising, he still had the will to fight. He stared straight at me and held out his saber. He was not acting out of desperation, nor had he lost his mind—he simply refused to give up. He was a true warrior, through and through.

I sensed he was still hiding something. If he intended to entertain me, then I was game. I extinguished my spear and drew my sword. I took my stance, the point of my blade trained on him as he cautiously closed the distance. Surely, he didn't think he could beat me with sword skills? He had to have something else up his sleeve.

I kept my eyes on him, not letting the slightest movement escape notice. Suddenly he halted, just out of my striking distance. He stayed there, frozen, and I suspected he wanted me to make the first move.

If that was his intention, then I would oblige. I leapt and, with one powerful swing, smashed the sword out of his hand. As his body lurched back, I kicked him again and sent him to the floor. There, I pinned him down with one foot.

Not a difficult victory. I didn't know what he'd been aiming for, but I'd thwarted his plan. So why, then, did alarm bells still seem to be ringing inside me?

Did he still have some secret tactic in mind? I wanted to look him directly in his single eye, to see what I might detect there, and the moment I leaned forward to do just that I saw his right hand give a hard jerk. Immediately, I sprang to the side. There was a flash, a bang, and something grazed my cheek and nicked my earlobe.

Dammit! I let my guard down!

I hit the floor, and as I rolled, I deployed a shield of light in case there was a second shot. The Black Dog was already up, smoke curling out of a gun concealed in his breastplate. He reached down and drew a handgun from the holster of the first orc I'd killed.

Once he saw I already had my shield up, though, he held back from firing and unsheathed a knife with his free hand. My attack would usually have been impossible to avoid, but he'd seen right through me; he could tell I was aiming to disarm him.

As I was getting up, the Black Dog dove at me, seeking to get around my shield, pointing the pistol in his left hand at my face. The black muzzle lined up with my pupil. I twisted my body with a violent wrench while repositioning the shield. Would I be fast enough?

The Black Dog pulled the trigger, but I was just a fraction of a second quicker. There was a shrill shriek as the bullet skimmed the edge of the shield. However, the gun spewed not only a bullet but a bright flash of gas, obscuring my vision.

I jumped back to put some distance between us. Not only was I momentarily blinded, but my ears were ringing too, compromising another of my senses. Relying almost solely on pure fighting instinct, I swung my left arm toward him.

Augh!

Pain raced through my arm, as if someone had thrust a hot poker against my flesh. I let loose a kick toward the spot where I believed his attack had come from. It wasn't a straight-on blow, but I had definitely connected with something. I hoped it would buy me a second or two in which to better regain myself.

I kept my guard up, and my shield facing forward, as my vision gradually returned. An afterimage of the flash still lingered, but I could now see through it. So, where was he?

The Black Dog was a short distance away, in a crouch with just a spent gun in one fist and a dagger in the other. Seeing I was ready to come at him again full force, he fell to his knees and raised his hands, his weapons clanging to the floor. He was finally out of tricks.

No—I saw from the fire blazing in his lone eye that he wasn't truly ready to give up. Gambling on the hope that I'd take him in alive, he was surely only going through the motions of surrendering for now, until some mode of escape or rescue presented itself to him later.

I heard a clatter from the stairs. Thankfully, it was the garrison, not more orcs. The guards immediately surrounded the Black Dog, and one of them slammed the orc with the butt end of his pike.

"Stop!" I commanded before he or the others could go any further. I'd been through so much to take this person in alive!

Still, the blow to his head had knocked the Black Dog unconscious, and as he collapsed, something round rolled out of the pouch he wore. This blue, gem-like object rolled along the complicated glowing patterns of the magic circle until it came to a rest at my feet.

The moment I picked it up, I felt something like a blessing suffuse me. It wasn't as if I'd heard a voice or seen a vision, but somehow I just *knew* where this sensation originated from. It had to do with the same unknown presence that kept sending me off to other worlds.

But why was I experiencing this sensation now? That entity had only ever blessed me for one reason: when I had succeeded in saving a world from its crisis. Was the blue gem itself the source of a world-threatening crisis, then?

I stared at it in contemplation. I didn't know what the Black Dog had intended to do with it, but he must have had some specific mission in mind, to brave infiltrating this place with so few troops. Perhaps the crisis only came into play when this stone and the Black Dog were paired together, like a bomb and a fuse.

If all this was true, I didn't know what my next step should be. However, my intuition guided me to a surprisingly simple answer. It hadn't even been a year since I'd arrived in this world. If I were to save it right here, right now, it would definitely be my record for the fastest I'd ever done this. I stared at the blue gemstone again, imagining that soon enough I'd be standing upon my own world again.

Well, if that was what was going to happen, I should get on with it.

In my right hand, I manifested a knife-sized spear of light. The simple answer that had come to me was this: if I shattered the gem, the crisis to this world would be ended.

And yet, how would things go if I chose not to break it? If the blue gem was the source of this world's crisis, would I be able to stay here as long as I wanted if I left it intact?

I'd played with this system before. For instance, I'd held off from finishing the demon lord so I could properly say goodbye to my comrades. By taking my fate into my own hands, might it be possible for me to remain in this world forever?

If the matter was left unresolved, though, a threat would always linger. No, I mustn't let myself be fooled by the devil's temptations. My conscience spoke up sternly. *Do you intend to just die one day in this world? Didn't you promise that girl you'd fight as a hero? Do you want to disappoint her? Quit it with these pointless thoughts. Hurry up and save the world, and go home.*

Oh, but doubts assailed me. Would breaking this mysterious object *truly* save humanity here? Perhaps they would be safer for a while, but by now, the orcs could already have broken through the fortress walls and driven the humans to extinction, even without the aid of this gem. The only reason they hadn't yet was that they felt such a campaign would be more trouble than it was worth. Breaking this object might only be delaying that extinction.

For guidance, I reached out with my thoughts to that unknown presence, but received no answer...as always.

Another of the conflicting voices inside me whispered temptingly: *What if by remaining here you could help build an even better future for this world? What if you can achieve a peace treaty with the orcs? And most importantly, if you stay here, you'll be able to fight forever!*

Oho, conscience. You sounded pretty noble for a minute there, until you became honest at the end. Not to mention contradictory.

Words Meg had spoken to me suddenly came to mind.

"You yourself could choose to live free, Hero."

I glanced at the Black Dog, who had regained consciousness. He was watching me with a glare that betrayed his indomitable fighting spirit, but he also seemed curious as to what I was thinking.

If I gave up resisting and just destroyed the gem, then all would be settled. But then, only those who didn't give up could ever really know freedom. No, I wasn't ready yet. I would experiment a bit with destiny. I could always give up later.

I stuffed the gem into my pocket and ordered the guards, "Tie him up, but listen…you aren't to kill him, no matter what."

In my head there arose a strange uproar. This was the first time the unseen entity had ever reacted in this way. I actually found it refreshing.

The night of orc raids came to a close. I yawned, only to grimace at the pain that brought, which only made it worse. The doctor priest who'd tended to me had said the bullet graze to my cheek might leave a scar. My left arm ached as well from having lashed out with it blindly only to connect with the Black Dog's knife. At least I'd inadvertently saved my own life by doing so.

After changing into fresh clothes and smearing my face with the sticky ointment the doctor priest had given me, I left my room to face a new day. A bit groggy from sleep, I looked into the sky just as Veralgon passed overhead, his white wings spread wide. Having been let loose without a rider, he now descended toward the dragon house. Even from a distance, I saw the red stains around his mouth, and I knew he'd gone on quite a rampage. Having been awakened last night by gunfire, he'd made a mess of the dragon house, and by morning, when his thrashing grew dangerously out of control, he'd finally been set free. The smell of orc blood had been too much for him to contain himself.

I stifled another yawn and headed to find Herbert. I needed to check the information I had on hand. He'd let me rest until the sun was high in the sky, so there apparently weren't any new issues to concern me.

The being that had sent me here had finally gone quiet. Its presence hadn't disappeared entirely, however. Perhaps it wanted to see what I intended to do. It needed to have faith in me, I thought. I was, after all, the hero who had already saved twelve worlds.

I found Herbert in front of the gate tower, receiving various reports.

"Oh, Hero! You came at just the right time. The scouts we sent into the valley have returned."

"Have you pieced these events together?"

"Yes, and it seems we fell for their plot hook, line, and sinker."

As it turned out, the torches in the valley had indeed only been a bluff, continuing to burn even after the beak-dog riders had retreated. Scouts sent out at daybreak had found nothing but a large number of torches atop stakes driven into the ground. It would only have taken a few members of the enemy team to light them all.

"It was wise of you to see through their true intentions, Hero."

"It was because you permitted me to act freely. Also, I didn't see through it completely. I just thought that if I had nothing better to do, I might as well prepare for the worst."

"And that ultimately saved us. We know now the underground chamber was their objective, but how did they learn about it?"

"We still need to confirm that. Did you send a messenger to the village?"

"Yes, they should be here soon."

Just then a ruckus broke out in the direction of the dragon house. I heard a dragon's roar, a human scream, then a number of shouted orders.

This was not good. Suspecting what had happened, I raced that way at top speed.

The dragon house of Dragonjaw Gate was near the plaza beyond the gate tower, on the path to the village. In front of it, a single white dragon spread his wings wide and let out an intimidating growl. The surrounding dragon keepers were attempting to lasso Veralgon, but his snapping jaws severed each rope. Nearby, a group of ten garrison soldiers nervously held their spears at the ready. Behind them, George stood protectively in front of Lily.

Veralgon roared, demanding the soldiers get out of the way. Elites that they were, they held their ground. They must've been exceedingly well trained. But this was no time to be impressed; I needed to help them. Fortunately, Veralgon's fire sack seemed to be empty, or else everyone might have already been burned alive.

"Oi! Veralgon! Stop!" I called out as I approached.

I needed to calm him, and fast. As agitated as he was, I figured I would need to mount him to take control and get him back into the dragon house. As I approached with this in mind, a tail came flying straight at me. I ducked beneath it and it passed over my head with a whoosh. I hadn't experienced anything like this since the first time I'd ridden him.

His rage likely stemmed from Lily. Despite all his tail flailing to keep me away, he never took his eyes off the orc. Veralgon was a clever dragon who'd never forgotten how his former rider had been killed by orcs, and thus he harbored a deep hatred for them.

I narrowly evaded several more lashes of his tail until I could cling to his back, presently without a saddle. His emotions flooded into me the moment I touched him, and I had to use all my mental fortitude to subdue them. Veralgon resisted this effort, stubbornly refusing to budge from the spot.

I called to George, "Get Lily to safety while I can still hold him back!"

George nodded and took Lily by the arm. Together with the ten guards, they timidly passed by me and the dragon I fought to restrain.

When Lily was out of sight, Veralgon finally regained his composure. He reluctantly lowered his resistance and handed control over to me. I heaved a relieved sigh. Still, I could tell his abhorrence of all things orc continued to eddy within him. He must have been considerably irritated to try to get rid of me too.

His eyes took in our surroundings. They overpowered even my own sense of vision. Still keeping a safe distance, the dragon keepers looked reluctant to make another attempt at handling him.

"Sorry, Your Excellency," one of them said. "But could you continue to calm him for just a bit longer?"

I understood their concern. I was reluctant to hand him over to them like this too.

"No worries. I'll take him on a flight. Please prepare a cow for him."

"Yes, sir."

From there, I led Veralgon away and into the sky. I let him fly freely for a while, then urged him to perform a series of acrobatics to burn off some steam. Of course, this was more than a little risky for me, without the benefit of a saddle or any safety gear.

When we returned to the dragon house at last, the keepers were waiting with plenty of raw meat. I could only hope that one cow was enough to improve his mood.

Once Veralgon was done feasting, I left him with the keepers and set off for Dragonjaw Gate's central tower.

I'd really gone through hell just now, blasted by icy winds while desperately clinging to the dragon. I could barely feel my face and hands, and I hoped I didn't come down with frostbite. As if I hadn't already felt bad enough from the previous night's battle! I would need to get the doctor priest to look at me again.

Resisting the temptation to go sit by a warm fireplace, I headed underground. George, Lily, and two guards were waiting for me in front of the dungeon.

"Sorry to keep you waiting," I told George. "That must have been terrifying. Are you all right?"

"Yes, Your Excellency. Thank you for rescuing us."

George and Lily bowed their heads.

"Well, thank you for protecting Lily. Can't lose her, now can we?"

My praise was sincere. George had stood up to Veralgon's terrifying glare to protect her. While he looked somewhat underwhelming, he was still the son of a great lord. The same blood as Thret's ran through his veins.

"Did you bring the dictionary and the stone slate?"

"Yes, sir… Right here," he said, producing the sage's book. The stone and chalk were in Lily's hands.

"Then let's go."

A sentry inserted a hefty key into the dungeon's main door and turned it. Once we were all inside, I heard the lock slide back into place.

"Where is the Black Dog?"

Another sentry inside stepped up to lead us. "He's being held in solitary confinement, in the farthest cell in the back. Follow me."

Two guards were stationed at the door of the farthest cell. Security was quite strict, though I could understand their concerns. Having expected us, one of them opened a peephole to peer inside, then took out a small key and opened the door.

The Black Dog sat with both hands bound with chains to the back wall. When he saw me enter his cell, his solitary eye gleamed with the same indomitable spirit as when he'd been captured. Then I saw his gaze grow even sharper. Fresh rage seemed to build in him, but why? I hadn't done anything yet that might have provoked him.

I turned and saw that George and Lily had entered the room behind me. Oh, so that was what it was. Anyone with a sense of justice would have become enraged to see one of their own kind, especially a young maiden, with a collar around their neck and being led by a chain like a dog.

The door shut behind George, and the guard relocked it.

"George, remove Lily's collar."

"Yes, sir."

Now, to get down to business. It was time to test the results of our language training, and I'd already decided on the basic approach. First, Lily would translate my spoken words into orcish by writing them on the chalkboard. Then, I would use the dictionary to decipher them. I hadn't taught Lily any of the language of the humans in this world. When possible, I tried not to let her see the dictionary either. On the off chance that she ever escaped, the less information she could pass on to the orcs, the better. The only words I had taught her were in Japanese, which other orcs could never make use of.

Then again, from overhearing George's daily conversations with our housekeeper and others, there was a good chance she had, in fact, picked up some of the words used by this world's humans but had kept them to herself. Lily was smart, after all. It was said that all humans captured by orcs were brutally killed, but no one knew if that were really the truth of the matter. Lily had communicated to me that she had never seen a captured human before, but I wondered if any of them had ever been taken prisoner and used by the orcs to study the human language, in the reverse of what I was doing. Well, if so, they hadn't used that knowledge to pursue a treaty.

But my thoughts were getting off track. I was here to interrogate the Black Dog.

I gestured to Lily, and she stepped forward and bowed to me.

I was about to get things started, but before I could speak, the Black Dog entered into a series of emphatic grunts. Whatever he'd said to Lily caused her eyes to widen. Wait, did they already know each other?

When Lily oinked back to him, sounding powerless, the Black Dog grunted sharply and critically. Whatever his words meant, they were intense. After several of these short exchanges, Lily collapsed on the spot and began bawling miserably. George squatted down beside her and began patting her on the back, but the tears wouldn't stop. How could she be of use to me like this?

The Black Dog switched his gaze to me, but upon seeing the reproach in my eyes, he awkwardly looked away, as if to say, *Ah, I've really done it now.*

At Dragonjaw Gate, in a lonely cell...

How much time had passed since the raid had failed? The Black Dog judged it couldn't have been that long. He suspected it was about time for the sun to rise, but there were no windows to confirm or deny this theory.

Bound with chains, he continued to reflect on his battle the night before. No matter how many times he went over it, he could only consider it a failure on his part. It seemed at first that everything had been going well. The enemy had fallen for their schemes and concentrated their forces on the decoy unit. Or had the humans set a trap of their own? Had the enemy seen through their plan from the start, pretending they had fallen for the scheme, while in reality lying in wait at the tower? Why else would the Demon King have been in readiness there? He was their greatest asset, and they would've certainly made use of him.

The Black Dog seethed when he thought of his fallen comrades and aquilup, yet he wasn't as angry at the enemy as he was with himself for his own carelessness. Even if he did recognize his failure, that didn't mean he was giving up. So long as he was alive, there would be a chance to redeem himself. Luckily, the humans *wanted* to keep him alive, even if he didn't know why. He had noticed during the battle that the Demon King had sought to take him in one piece. In any case, the Black Dog convinced himself his chance would come, and he'd wait for it. Next time, he wouldn't fail. Still, it took quite a bit of willpower to keep from falling into despair at this present situation.

Suddenly, in the distance he heard a heavy door being opened and then closed. This was followed by multiple footsteps, echoing in the hallway as they came in this direction. His body was bound, but his wits were sharp.

When the door to his cell opened it was the Demon King who entered, as expected. He had suffered a shallow gunshot wound to the face. The Black Dog felt gratified knowing it was he who had inflicted that mark.

Next came a small human male, holding a length of chain. At the other end of the chain, a captive young orc woman entered into view. She had not been given shoes despite the winter cold, and she wore nothing but thin, shoddy clothing.

What terrible treatment! The Black Dog was enraged. What were they planning to do with this maiden?

He knew of an interrogation method that involved forcing the prisoner to watch helplessly as a friend was tortured. This often proved more effective than torturing the subject of the interrogation himself. He imagined and feared what was to come. His one eye glared at the Demon King.

Surprisingly, he thought he saw hesitation in the Demon King's face, as he no doubt guessed the source of the Black Dog's fury. Once the door was closed behind them, the smaller human undid the maiden's collar. The woman's manner surprised him. She didn't seem anxious in the slightest, simply raising her chin to make the removal of her collar easier. She must have trusted the humans considerably. On closer inspection, the Black Dog thought her complexion was good, and she didn't seem underfed or injured. Perhaps she was actually being treated properly, after all.

As he continued to watch her, the Black Dog thought he recognized her face from somewhere. She stepped forward and bowed. It was the elegant gesture of someone accustomed to bowing before a noble. The moment he saw this, the Black Dog recognized her. This woman was definitely the personal maid of the margrave's daughter. Seeking to confirm this, he spoke to her urgently in their orcish language, and she gave the affirmative. What fantastic luck!

If the maid was alive, that meant there was a chance the daughter was alive as well. The possibility was wonderful news. The margrave would be uplifted to hear it, and it might even give him the strength to overcome his illness.

Ignoring the others in the cell, the Black Dog hammered her with questions.

"Where is your mistress?"

"I don't know."

"Is she alive?"

"I don't know."

"When did you last see her?"

"Three years ago. We parted as soon as we were captured."

"Where did you last see her?"

"At the slave market."

"Why didn't you remain with her?"

"We were separated by force."

"Why do you help humans now—have you no shame?!"

Under his harsh chastisement, the maid finally crumpled in tears. The small human drew close and attempted to console her. Listening to her piteous wails, the Black Dog finally regained his self-control. What could this weak young lady have done differently under those conditions? No doubt she had overcome many hardships and struggled desperately to survive, her situation much like the one he found himself in now. Why had he spat such venom at her?

As he awkwardly fiddled with his chains, his gaze met that of the Demon King. Unable to endure the rebuke in his eyes, the Black Dog turned away.

It took some time for Lily to calm down. I considered proceeding without her, using purely the written word to communicate with the captive, but decided to wait for her. For one thing, I was limited to the words in the dictionary and had absolutely no understanding of syntax. I could apply a bit of conjecture when reading orcish, and context certainly helped, but that was of no use when it was me doing the writing. I had much yet to learn.

Perhaps it was cowardice, but I was also reluctant to undo the Black Dog's chains in order to have him write. Yes, I had held back in our battle, but no matter how you looked at it, he had managed to drive the hero himself into a corner. Plus, there was the risk that he might kill himself given the chance, rather than cooperate with the enemy.

Lily had finally calmed, the overall tension in the cell had dispersed, and I gave my orc assistant the first words to translate.

"What, last night, attack, purpose?"

I emphasized each term, but occasionally she held up a finger, this being the signal when she didn't know a certain word. She had raised the third finger. She didn't know the word "attack." Our language lessons mostly dealt with everyday objects and activities, so we hadn't gotten far in other areas. I searched out "attack" in the sage's notes and wrote the appropriate orcish word in chalk.

She seemed satisfied, and with the message complete, conveyed it to the Black Dog.

His answer was very short. Lily wrote it on the board and showed me. I was actually thankful for how short it was because just finding one word in the dictionary could be time-consuming enough. If his reply had been long-winded, who could say how long it would take to interpret it?

The words this time were "wall" and "break." The wall obviously meant Dragonjaw Gate. They had come to destroy the fortress. But how?

"How, break?"

I passed my words on to Lily, who conveyed them to the Black Dog, who passed his answer on to Lily, who—oh, what a process!

In essence, the exchange went as follows...

Question: "How did you intend to break the wall?"

Answer: "I heard it would fall to pieces if the blue orb was placed in the center of the glowing room."

The blue orb was clearly the gem that had fallen out of his bag. I produced it from my pocket to show him.

Question: "Is this the orb?"

Answer: "Yes."

As I thought. But where did it come from?

Question: "Where did you find it?"

Answer: "Researchers found it in the ruins. I do not know anything else."

Question: "How did you know how to get to the underground chamber?"

Answer: "The researchers found a book. I do not know anything else."

In the ruins of the ancients, orcish researchers had obtained information about Dragonjaw Gate's layout, as well as a means of destroying the fortress. That was far too convenient. In fact, it seemed like our fates had been threaded together. Had their discovery of this information been the catalyst that had summoned me to this world?

I recalled details that supported his story. The report I'd found in his bag contained writing in ancient script as well as orcish. When I'd showed it to Worion, he'd surmised the researchers had copied the contents directly from ancient documents. Rigel had once discovered a book about the magic circle in the ancient capital, so it wouldn't be strange if other historical documents and books remained. I stared probingly into the Black Dog's eye. He didn't seem to be lying, but I wasn't convinced he was telling the truth.

With a deep sigh, I stared at the ceiling, already exhausted. I'd expended so much effort to obtain so little information. I could tell both Lily and the Black Dog were worn thin from the process themselves.

At this point, I had no way to determine what was true and what wasn't. I hoped the sage could help me in understanding the text in the documents I'd obtained. For now, I was done here.

I knocked on the cell door to summon the sentries. One of them opened the peephole, saw all was in order within, and let us out. Further on, we were allowed to exit through the dungeon's gate.

By the time we stepped outside the sun was already setting, and I took a deep breath of cold, clean air. The air back there in the dungeon had been stagnant and unhealthy. I wanted the

Black Dog to be able to breathe this fresh air too, but he would need to put up with the dungeon for a little while longer.

The next day, I was awakened by a banging at my door. I hurried to get dressed and opened it to find Herbert standing there, his face pale. The captain himself had come to see me; no wonder the pounding had been so severe.

"I don't know how I can apologize," he began, lowering his head.

"What happened?"

"The Black Dog got away."

I tried to look as surprised as possible. "From the dungeons? How?"

"That's the thing—we just don't know. The soldiers on watch were all rendered unconscious, and they didn't know how. The key was stolen, and now his cell is empty."

Ah, the infamous Black Dog, seemingly with powers beyond those of any ordinary orc.

Herbert continued, "I stationed our finest men to watch him, yet he still escaped easily. And after all you went through to take him alive!" He looked at me as if with pity, not just because my efforts had apparently been in vain, but because of my battle-worn appearance. To make matters worse, I couldn't shave because of that ointment-coated groove in my cheek.

"You're not to blame," I reassured him. "No one could have expected this. The Black Dog truly is formidable, isn't he?"

My consoling words seemed inadequate, as I saw him clench his fist in frustration.

"Did you report the Black Dog's capture to the capital yet?"

"No, we haven't. Pending the results of your interrogation of him, so far all we've done is report that we successfully repelled the enemy."

"I see. In that case, you don't need to report this."

Herbert looked at me in disbelief. "I couldn't possibly do that! It would completely erase your achievements! I'll take full responsibility for this failure, so please—"

"The safety of the underground chamber is proof enough of my achievements. Eventually, I'll leave this world. I have no interest in territory or assets." I placed a hand on his shoulder. "All I really need is strong allies if I'm to save this world. You placed your best men as sentries, correct? If you report this, they may face punishment—and certainly disgrace—and I don't want that. I don't want it for you either."

Herbert trembled with emotion. "What gracious words, Hero! I'll never forget the debt I owe you."

"I'll be counting on you. I'm sure I'll need your courage again someday."

As we exchanged a firm handshake, my face didn't betray to Herbert that a presence clamored inside my head, just as it had when I had decided not to shatter the enigmatic blue gem.

Was the entity weaker than I had believed? After the other night, I had been prepared to be punished for my act—or rather, inaction—by having my hero's powers stripped from me. And yet, nothing of the sort had happened.

The Black Dog dragged his feet across the wasteland, leaning his weight on a walking stick. He hadn't gotten a wink of sleep since before the attack, and he hadn't ingested anything save for the meager water offered to him in his cell. Tired, starving, and thirsty, his body was at its limit. He felt the urge to collapse and sleep on the spot, but he knew if he did, he would not rise again.

The only rest he allowed himself came in the form of standing in one place from time to time, propped up by his stick. During one of these brief breaks, he turned to look behind him. There, a mountain range loomed like a vast wall, and the massive water dragon carved into its face lorded over the plains. Back when he had sealed the valley, he had viewed this scene enough times to grow sick of it. In his cell, he'd assumed he would never see it again. He had told himself he would eventually escape one way or another, but in the depths of his heart, he'd believed he would never leave that cell alive. And yet, liberation had indeed come, all too easily.

The one who had guided him out of the dungeon had been, of all people, the Demon King himself.

Hours after the interrogation, in the dead of night, the Demon King had appeared again, accompanied by the orc maid on her chain, and led the Black Dog out of the damp dungeon. Along the way, he had seen that all the guards lay unconscious, and he'd realized the Demon King was acting on his own discretion.

When they parted outside the fortress, the Demon King tossed the blue gem back to him and, with the maid's help, told him, "I set you free. Never let go of that."

The Black Dog didn't know what that meant, but he understood the Demon King's seriousness as he said it. Mysteriously, the sentiment was potent enough to easily step over the line drawn between their races. If he was to be released so easily, though, why had the Demon King gone through such effort to capture him? Had the answers he'd received during the interrogation been all he sought?

Upon reflection, the Black Dog couldn't recall having said anything significant. Even if some important information had been contained in his words, that would still be no reason to free him. He especially couldn't comprehend why the gemstone that could destroy the wall had simply been handed back to him. Judging by the seriousness of the Demon King's demeanor, the jewel couldn't have turned out to be worthless junk. The Black Dog simply couldn't get a read on him.

Whatever the human's motives, the Black Dog found his release to be a cause for celebration. While he had failed to bring down the wall, he had still learned valuable information—about the Demon King, a former maid serving as an interpreter, and the margrave's daughter. He could now bring this information back to the margrave's city. Whether it would change their interactions with humans henceforth was for the higher-ups to ponder.

The Black Dog wondered how that lazy son would react. There was a strong chance he wouldn't believe him. His report on his confrontation with the Demon King and his subsequent release would surely sound like complete nonsense.

No matter what, the possibility that the margrave's daughter was alive would certainly be treated as good news. He needed to get to him and tell him.

He turned from the mountains, back to the desolate expanse of the north. He continued on with renewed determination, but the margrave's city was far away yet, the hills on the horizon seeming to never get any closer. His feet grew heavier step by step, and his pace continued to lag.

As he walked, he thought back to the black aquilup he had lost in the battle. How reassuring it would be if his beloved partner of many years were here to carry him. Only now was the loss beginning to set in, and he had lost far more than that. Not a single one of the friends he had first set out with remained. If any of the others from the mercenary brigade had survived, they would have retreated to the margrave's city, as the Black Dog had ordered them to do if he didn't return from his mission. Their short-range riding guns wouldn't be enough against dragons when the sun rose.

His equipment had all been confiscated, and the Black Dog had been ejected into the wasteland with nothing more than the clothes on his back. All he had left was his life, and even that felt like it was weathering away. The reclaimed northern lands had become vast, uninhabitable expanses, and it would take several days to reach even the nearest village. How was he to achieve that without food and water? Yet on he trudged.

A single pebble was all it took for his heart to fall to pieces.

It wasn't a special stone by any means, save for the fact that it happened to lie where he brought his foot down. Its pressure against his sole caused his body to jerk a little, but in his weakened state, that was enough to throw him off balance. He fell facedown, his arms lacking even the power to break his fall. He couldn't push himself back up or even roll onto his back. So this was the end, then... His news would go undelivered. Lying there, he closed his eye and deeply breathed in the smell of dirt, ready to submit to endless sleep.

Then a familiar whistle reached his ears. The whistle was the one aquilup riders used to communicate with one another. He had no allies out here, though, so it had to be that his fallen comrades were welcoming him to the other side. When he pressed his ear to the ground, he heard the sound of aquilup claws approaching at a rapid pace. They stopped just short of him. The reaper was here.

He opened his eye to look up and see what form the reaper had assumed, but it was not death who greeted him. It was, rather, a lanky orc with a familiar face, a face that shouldn't have been here. It belonged to the subordinate to whom he'd entrusted command of the main force, before the mission began.

"What, you died too?" the Black Dog said to him, despairing. If this cautious and capable orc had been killed, then the whole unit must have suffered devastating losses.

"What are you talking about?" his subordinate said. "I'm right as rain."

The lanky orc scoffed as if to say, *Don't lump us together.* It took some time for the Black Dog to realize what was going on.

"You're...alive."

"Yes, as you can see," the man replied. He dismounted his aquilup, lifted the Black Dog off the ground, and gave him his canteen. A comforting sloshing could be heard from inside the metal canister. "Drink up."

Somehow revitalized, the Black Dog downed all its contents. When he could catch his breath again, he asked, "Why are you here? I ordered you to retreat."

The lanky orc shrugged. "You didn't come back, but I knew you weren't going to bite the dust that easily, Boss. I thought maybe you'd lost your aquilup and were having a hard time rejoining us, so I figured I should search the area."

"What about my orders?"

"Sorry about that, but without you around I wouldn't want to stay in this line of work. I know it was risky, but I've been skulking around the forests so the dragons don't find me. What about you, Boss? You're a fine target, walking around in the middle of the plains."

The Black Dog had no response to that.

"Well, you're safe, and that's all that matters. The others will be here soon. Look."

He gestured around, and sure enough, other aquilup riders bounded toward them from their hiding spots. When they saw the Black Dog was alive, they all gave a cheer, the tusks in their widened mouths gleaming.

"As long as you're alive, boss, everything will work out. Next time, it's victory!"

With that, he lifted the Black Dog up onto his saddle. The aquilup groaned in protest, but after its owner rubbed it on the beak, it begrudgingly accepted the new rider. He jumped up in front of his captain, and this time it was the extra weight that caused the aquilup to grumble.

"Let's get out of here," the lanky orc said.

Before the Black Dog knew it, he was surrounded by a herd of aquilup riders, apparently all the remaining survivors of their team. Their numbers had dwindled since the start of the mission, but the faces that surrounded him were bright. Of course they were; they had finally found the leader they so admired. They watched the Black Dog expectantly, awaiting his orders.

He called up his deepest reserve of power and roared, "Troops—pull out!"

"Yes, sir!" they all shouted back.

They set out toward the south. They had a message to deliver to the margrave.

BONUS STORY

MY FOURTH WORLD: MEETING THE MAGICIAN SIBLINGS

"HEY, WILL...do you think that'll do it?" a girl asked, her voice echoing through the empty basement.

The boy named Will ignored the girl, instead focusing on the complex patterns he was drawing on the stone floor. His fingertips had turned white with chalk. They were both in their mid-teens.

"Hey, Will! Listen to me!"

"Can it," he finally replied irritably.

The girl's cheeks puffed up at her brother's indifference. She carefully lifted the hem of her robe so it wouldn't drag and erase the lines she had drawn. Then, poised on the tips of her toes, she carefully stepped to a corner of the room.

Her brother was usually decent toward her, but not when he was immersed in the arcane arts. At times like these, even the slightest impediment was enough to make him snap. To make matters worse, both his master and his fellow pupils saw this kind of intensity as a good thing for mages to possess, so no one scolded him about it. Still, his sister felt this was why he would always be alone.

At this rate, my brother will be joining their ranks in no time, the girl thought as she took a seat.

All the junk that had formerly filled the basement had been moved outside the day before. This alone had been an arduous undertaking for the both of them. Now the floor was covered with bizarre and convoluted symbols—the fruits of their labor. These were not merely decorative designs; each symbol had its own meaning and purpose, and together they formed a magic circle. Not even a single line of it could be off, or else the whole of the drawing would lose its effect...or worse, run of control.

If the latter happened, and they lost control of the magic circle, God only knew what might occur. One of the senior pupils had once made a minor mistake, and thereafter, he had been forced to live with an uncanny flower blooming from his head. No matter how many times he pruned it, it would be back the next day, and he would be assailed by unimaginable pain should he try to uproot it.

Many saw her brother as some genius magician. He had been scouted by Imall the Archmagus, and in only a few years, he would go on to shock everyone for having picked up many of the master's secrets. Every magician who knew of him also knew that the day he would stand shoulder to shoulder with Master Imall was not far away.

At the moment, Will was attempting to summon a form of spirit known as a helper demon. It was the most elementary summoning spell. The girl had often observed these small, humanoid figures assisting the senior disciples. Will intended to use the demon to search for his master's precious ring, which he had secretly made off with the other night and then lost.

One would think completing a spell of this type would be no problem at all for her genius brother. However, even after he had finished his work, Will checked it over again and again. There was a reason he was being so cautious—summoning arts were the only thing Master Imall wasn't prepared to teach him. Will's level of magical knowledge and ability was still growing and constantly in flux, making for a kind of instability. If he attempted a summoning in such a state, there was no telling what might be called forth.

But Will wasn't one to back down just because he was told to. He'd sneaked into the library without being seen, flipped through the books on summoning, and studied the techniques on his own. With the master and all the other apprentices away today, it was the perfect opportunity for him to put his knowledge to the test.

Once she felt he was done reviewing his own work, his sister called, "Hey, Will, make sure you check my part too."

"Yeah, sorry about that, Marie. I'll be right over."

His tone was softer than before, but Marie still sullenly turned her face from him.

Paying her attitude no mind, Will stooped down and began inspecting the sections of the composition she had been tasked with drawing. Marie watched him from the corner of her eye.

"Thank you," he said. "It's perfect."

Once he'd finished his inspection, he stepped carefully to Marie and ruffled her hair.

"Stop it! You're making a mess of it. Oh, I won't forget this!"

Ignoring her protests, Will made his way to the center of the magic circle.

"Now, let's begin. Marie, could you move back more?" As he said this, his face was not that of a teenage boy, but of a true magician.

Will placed his hands on the central chalk lines and began to chant a spell. His palms exuded a pale blue luminescence, which slowly spread across the floor along the many lines that formed the circle. When the uncanny light had fully outlined the drawing, he chanted the last section of the spell that would complete the ritual.

"Come to me, my tiny servant! Heed my words, and find what was lost in the woods!"

All the circle's light concentrated at a point before his eyes, flickering as it formed into a small humanoid shape. His tense posture relaxed somewhat as he became convinced of his success. The next moment, though, something seemed off.

The glowing figure, nearly fully constructed, began to waver and grow larger. Something had gone wrong, and Marie knew it. What was manifesting in this world was definitely not a helper demon, but something more powerful, more sinister.

"Will! You have to stop the ritual!"

"I can't—it's already taking form!"

What had once been a hazy outline of light now floated before them with definitive physical form.

"Marie! Run!"

But it was too late. By the time her brother screamed, the being was already there in the room with them.

Appearance-wise, it was simply a boy barely older than themselves, yet the figure carried a thick aura of death.

Will had to squeeze out every last drop of courage to ask, "Wh-who are you?"

The boy answered, "I am a hero. I am here to save the world."

That proclamation couldn't have sounded further from the truth. In the first place, they hadn't heard that the world was in some great danger. In Marie's eyes, it looked like this boy himself was the calamity.